Housebuilding For Children

Written, photographed, and illustrated by

Les Walker

Preface by Nonny Hogrogian

The Overlook Press
Lewis Hollow Road
Woodstock, New York 12498

First edition 1977
Published by
The Overlook Press Inc.
Lewis Hollow Road
Woodstock, New York 12498
Copyright © 1977 by Les Walker

790
WAL
c. 1

PLAY

ISBN # 0-87951-059-5
Library of Congress Catalog Card Number 76-47220

Printed in the USA

Table of Contents

To my grandfather, Christopher Walker, the first housebuilder I ever knew.

Special thanks to: Ian and Alice Bernstein of the Woodstock Children's Center for their inspiration, the housebuilding crew for their patience, the parents of the children for their understanding, Allan Mitchell for the use of his darkroom, the town of Woodstock, N.Y., for the use of their dump, the Woodstock Building Supply Company for their cooperation, and Sunfrost Farms of Woodstock for the orange crates.

Preface

Architecture has held a great fascination for me since I discovered Frank Lloyd Wright's work many years ago — and, I suppose, even longer ago than that, when I put together my own little hideaways in and around my childhood home.

But I never thought I could build one.

The first home my husband and I bought was an old, old house that was built when this country was first settled. It was built in the post and beam house technique. Much of it needed work but the foundation work from two hundred years ago stood as firmly as it did when the house was first built. We hired professional help to do the repair work so we could live in it, and it was a wonderful house.

But we have often talked about a special house, our own home that we would design that would be just right for our particular needs. It never seemed possible that we could do it ourselves, until I read this book by Les Walker.

It is concise, clear and easy to follow. The instructions and drawings are beautifully executed and the photographs of the children working are wonderful to behold.

Since we too are children in the world of housebuilding, the book is also for us; and it makes me feel that someday we can build our own special home.

I have already tried the picture frame and it worked.

I'm ready for the toolbox and tugboat.

What more can I say? The book is a wonderful experience in reading and looking, but I want to go the next step, which is to gather the materials, set up my workshop and begin.

Nonny Hogrogian

Introduction

My most vivid childhood memories, strangely perhaps, go back to building houses. I remember how, when I was about nine, I spent two days lugging home the parts of an old discarded furnace to add a cast-iron wing to my already-half-built pine and plywood house. That house was a beauty! It was two stories high and growing all the time. It had a small living room, a kitchen/dining area, and a relatively large vestibule. The bedroom was upstairs, if you could manage the rope ladder. And if you wanted to take a chance with your life, there was a lookout deck. I still remember the oil cloth on the walls and the hundreds of mis-hammered bent nails sticking out of every wall.

I loved my house, but our little one-quarter-acre grassy lot wasn't about to include *both* my parents' staid two-and-one-half-story, tudor-style brick house *and* my expanding, wobbly little junk-style shed. Especially since mine was leaning against theirs! My parents were tolerant people but once I started building my cast-iron wing, the aesthetics of the whole structure became unbearable even for them. I'll never forget their expressions — totally aghast yet contrite at having to tamper with their energetic son's aspirations.

There were always new single-family houses going up near our home and I soon found that I spent much of my time there during the day, scrounging waste materials for new house ideas and having some fun with the housebuilders. These sites were special places for me at night, too. I'll never forget the smell of a freshly framed wood house and the wonder of whether I would ever be good enough or big enough to build one. Why were my houses always so off-center and wobbly?

Years later after I'd become an architect — a Yale graduate with his own New York office, and even a professor at City College — I discovered that the more buildings I designed (or helped to get designed), the more frustrated I became. I still wanted to build!

So I finally moved to the country and immediately set about to build a house.

Here's a picture of the first house that I designed and built.

As I built it, I remember thinking, "What have I been doing all my life? This is such a pleasure." It took patience and desire but it was do-able! So easy, in fact, that I'm sure that with just a little bit of housebuilding experience and knowledge as a child, I would have had an even better time when I was nine.

So, this book is written for young people who want to build houses just as older people do. I designed six small houses that would educate children in the different "real-life" ways of building houses. While writing, I always remembered my experiences at a similar age. I remembered the desire to build a good, solid house and I didn't forget my frustration at having my early constructions sway in the wind.

Much to my surprise, about a year ago Ian Bernstein of the Woodstock Children's Center called me and asked me if I wanted to teach a carpentry class to 10 seven to nine year olds. I panicked at first, but I soon remembered my own housebuilding childhood and decided to take on the challenge. Ian went along with my idea of having the class build an actual house!

At first, most of the children could saw and hammer but had no concept of how to plan. When I realized this and began to relate it to their model-making abilities (step-by-step plans), we began to get going. We divided into four groups, each responsible for one wall of a four-sided house. Once the walls were built, each group decided where to put the windows and doors, and then they built them. Then we had a wall-fastening group, a foundation group, and a roof group. We framed our house in six hours! Step-by-step methods were the key.

I was happily amazed at their capabilities as they slowly gained housebuilding experience. They had framed a house and it looked exactly like a miniature balloon frame structure. There was no doubt about it; I could take this group, photograph it as the members built six houses and, hopefully, with this book, make an interesting contribution to the housebuilding nine year olds of the world.

1. ONCE UPON A TIME THERE WAS A LONG THIN SNAKE WHO LIVED IN A LONG THIN HOUSE.

2. HE MARRIED A SHORT FAT SOW WHO LIVED IN A SHORT FAT HOUSE.

3. THE LONG THIN SNAKE COULD NOT GET COMFORTABLE IN THE SHORT FAT SOW'S SHORT FAT HOUSE.

4. THE SHORT FAT SOW COULD NOT GO THROUGH THE DOORWAY OF THE LONG THIN SNAKE'S LONG THIN HOUSE.

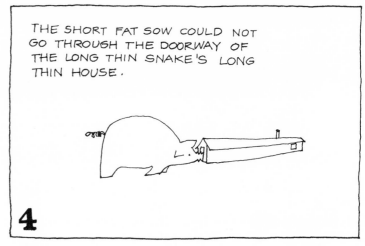

5. SO THEY BUILT A NEW HOUSE.

6. AND LIVED HAPPILY EVER AFTER.

The Housebuilding Crew

Here they are. The hard-working housebuilding crew with the tools used in building the houses throughout this book. The crew was made up of four girls and six boys who live in Woodstock, New York, all of whom attended the Woodstock Children's Center. We worked for two hours on Tuesday and Thursday afternoons after school, and four hours on Saturdays. A tough schedule but we wanted to be able to finish a different house every week!

Most of the time we worked hard and well but sometimes things got out of hand and I would turn into the "Krazed Kiddie Killer." The boys would pretend they were the "Banana Splits," and the girls would become the "Bionic Women." We'd drop our tools and go insane for a while. What a crew! But we managed to get the whole job finally done.

Adam Traum 10

Benjy Siegel 7

March Sadowitz 8

Lila Browne 7

Julie Bernstein 9½

Josh Browne 8
Tako Vos 9
Tommy Chasteen 9½

Jess Walker 7½

Zoë Siegel 8

Chapter 1
A Guide For Your Parents and Teacher

Construction on a house can't begin until a carpenter arrives on the site with all the tools and necessary materials. Anyone can learn to be a carpenter with the help of this book and lots of practice. But you'll need some help in getting the tools and materials to your housebuilding site.

If your parents or teacher read this book with you some afternoon, getting started will be easier.

Step 1: Buying Your Tools

It's very important to buy tools you can handle. If they're too heavy, too large, or not sharp enough, you'll find that some of the fun is gone. However, if they're the right size and weight, and they work well, it will add to the fun of carpentering.

The crosscut saw is the most critical tool. It must be sharp and have a blade that does not exceed 14 inches. Several companies make what is called a "Tool Box Saw," the perfect size. This saw is used by adults but is small enough to fit into a tool box. The hammer must weigh between seven and ten ounces and should be relatively small in size. A good hardware store will carry many different weighted hammers. Every other tool, including the keyhole saw, can be standard size. Your parents or teacher may want to buy these tools for their use or they may want to let you use theirs but it's best to assemble your own and have you responsible for them.

Here's a minimum list of tools you'll need to build the houses illustrated in Chapter Five. These are the lightest, safest, least expensive tools for the job.

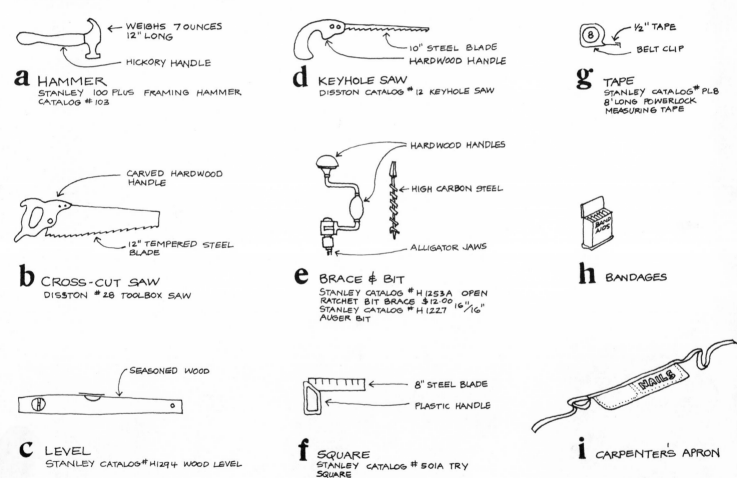

a HAMMER
STANLEY 100 PLUS FRAMING HAMMER
CATALOG # 103
— WEIGHS 7 OUNCES 12" LONG
— HICKORY HANDLE

b CROSS-CUT SAW
DISSTON # 28 TOOLBOX SAW
CARVED HARDWOOD HANDLE
12" TEMPERED STEEL BLADE

c LEVEL
STANLEY CATALOG # H1294 WOOD LEVEL
SEASONED WOOD

d KEYHOLE SAW
DISSTON CATALOG # 12 KEYHOLE SAW
10" STEEL BLADE
HARDWOOD HANDLE

e BRACE & BIT
STANLEY CATALOG # H1253A OPEN RATCHET BIT BRACE $12.00
STANLEY CATALOG # H1227 16"/16" AUGER BIT
HARDWOOD HANDLES
HIGH CARBON STEEL
ALLIGATOR JAWS

f SQUARE
STANLEY CATALOG # 501A TRY SQUARE
8" STEEL BLADE
PLASTIC HANDLE

g TAPE
STANLEY CATALOG # PL8 8' LONG POWERLOCK MEASURING TAPE
½" TAPE
BELT CLIP

h BANDAGES

i CARPENTERS' APRON

SEE THE APPENDIX FOR THE TOOL MANUFACTURER'S ADDRESSES

Step 2: Buying Your Materials

Have your parents or teacher order and have delivered from your lumber yard the complete materials for your workshop and the house you've chosen to build from Chapter Five. Make sure you're home when they're delivered so you can have them unloaded in a safe place.

For your workshop

At the beginning of the "Setting Up Your Workshop" chapter, you'll find all the materials you'll need. If you can't order the four concrete blocks from your local lumber yard, you may be able to get them at a local brick yard.

For your house

At the beginning of each house illustrated in Chapter Five, you'll find a listing of all the materials you'll need to construct your house. Before you order, ask for a cost estimate to make sure you have enough money to pay for them.

Getting Help

As mentioned before, it's best to read this book cover to cover with a parent or teacher, to fully understand what goes into building a house. As you read, make sure you understand how to use the tools illustrated in Chapter Three. Then, after you've bought the tools, ask a parent or teacher to watch you practice with them until you feel comfortable with them. Pay particular attention to the saw — the source of cuts, and the hammer — the source of bruises. If there are any questions about the use of a tool, re-read Chapter Three or ask a good local carpenter for help.

Check out your workshop after it has been built. Make sure it's rigid. If your workbench is outside, make sure your housebuilding tools are covered by the plastic sheet. Put something heavy over it, like rocks, to make sure it doesn't blow away. Check to see that your tools never get wet. Observe the work rules listed in Chapter Two.

Get criticism from your parents or teacher about the quality of the work you do on the practice projects. Can you saw better or nail straighter? Are the dimensions accurate and is the project straight and true? Ask for direction about how your work can be improved.

As you read through the book, carefully review the tasks you'll have to perform to build the house you've chosen. Keep asking questions until you feel you fully understand.

Chapter 2
Setting Up Your Workshop

After you've chosen your building site, the first thing you'll need is a place to work, your "workshop," in other words. It will be the center of activity for everything that relates to the building of your house.

This chapter illustrates a simple way of setting up a pleasant, well-ordered place to work that will help organize all your tools and plans.

Step 1: Buying the Materials

Ask your parents or teacher to call the lumber yard to order and have delivered the materials you'll need to build your workshop. They are all listed below. Try to stop off at the local printer and Xerox the pages from this book that show how to build the house you've chosen. You'll want to nail these plans to the back of your workbench so that you can see them at any time.

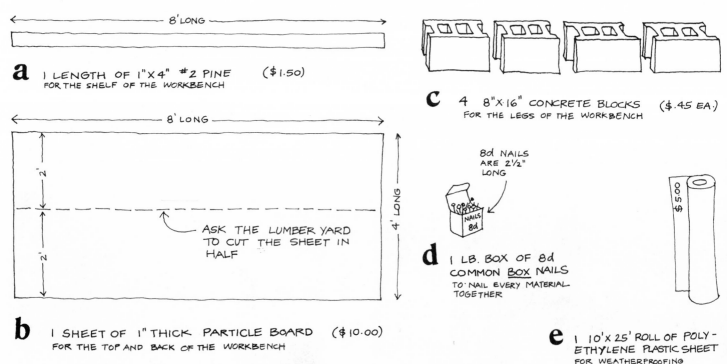

a 1 LENGTH OF 1"X 4" #2 PINE ($1.50)
FOR THE SHELF OF THE WORKBENCH

8' LONG

b 1 SHEET OF 1" THICK PARTICLE BOARD ($10.00)
FOR THE TOP AND BACK OF THE WORKBENCH

2' 2' 4' LONG

ASK THE LUMBER YARD TO CUT THE SHEET IN HALF

c 4 8"X 16" CONCRETE BLOCKS ($.45 EA.)
FOR THE LEGS OF THE WORKBENCH

8d NAILS ARE 2½" LONG

NAILS 8d

d 1 LB. BOX OF 8d COMMON BOX NAILS
TO NAIL EVERY MATERIAL TOGETHER

$5.00

e 1 10'X 25' ROLL OF POLY-ETHYLENE PLASTIC SHEET
FOR WEATHERPROOFING

Step 2: Building the Workbench

It's best to set up your workbench outside, near your site. But if it's too cold or wet, and if you have the space, you may want to set up indoors. You can always take your workbench apart by removing the nails and rebuild it outside. Here are the plans for building your workbench.

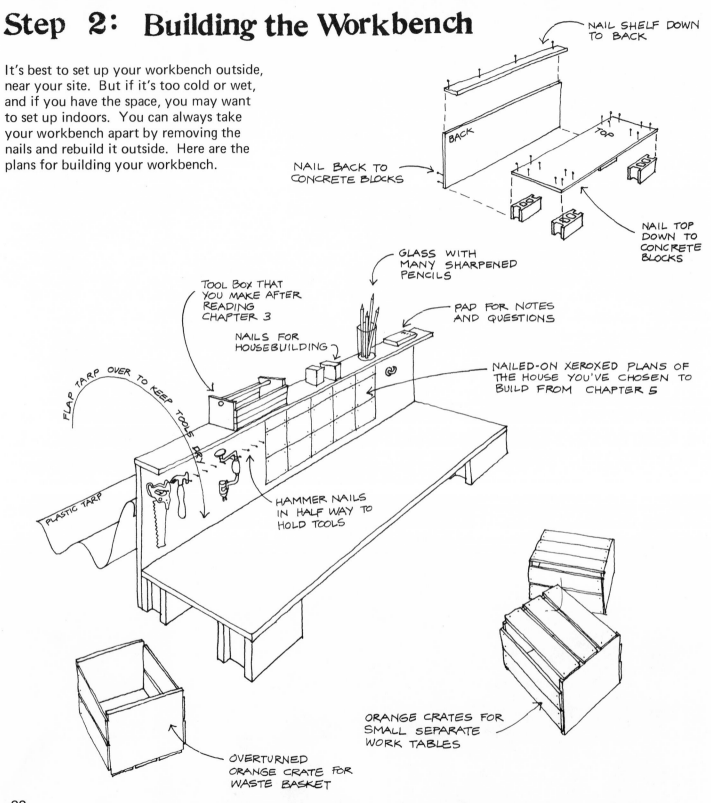

NAIL SHELF DOWN TO BACK

NAIL BACK TO CONCRETE BLOCKS

BACK

TOP

NAIL TOP DOWN TO CONCRETE BLOCKS

TOOL BOX THAT YOU MAKE AFTER READING CHAPTER 3

NAILS FOR HOUSEBUILDING

GLASS WITH MANY SHARPENED PENCILS

PAD FOR NOTES AND QUESTIONS

NAILED-ON XEROXED PLANS OF THE HOUSE YOU'VE CHOSEN TO BUILD FROM CHAPTER 5

FLAP TARP OVER TO KEEP TOOLS DRY

PLASTIC TARP

HAMMER NAILS IN HALF WAY TO HOLD TOOLS

ORANGE CRATES FOR SMALL SEPARATE WORK TABLES

OVERTURNED ORANGE CRATE FOR WASTE BASKET

Step 3: Storing Your Housebuilding Materials

As the materials for your house are unloaded from the truck, you should carry them to your building site. If some of the materials are too heavy, ask a friend to help you.

As soon as you get all the materials to your site, level them on strips or blocks of wood to make sure they don't warp. It's a good idea to cover the materials with a plastic sheet to keep them dry. It is very hard to saw or drill wet wood.

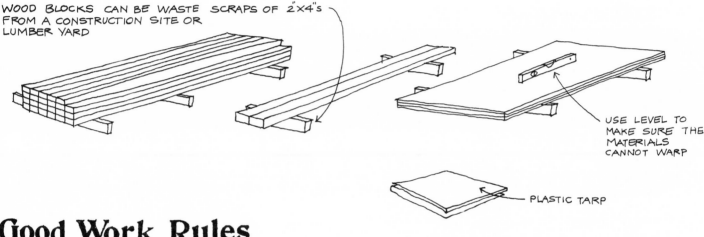

WOOD BLOCKS CAN BE WASTE SCRAPS OF 2"x4"s FROM A CONSTRUCTION SITE OR LUMBER YARD

USE LEVEL TO MAKE SURE THE MATERIALS CANNOT WARP

PLASTIC TARP

Good Work Rules

1. Every night put all your tools into your tool box and take them inside to keep them from getting rusty, unless you protect them with the plastic sheet.

2. Every night clean up your site and workbench, putting unusable pieces of wood and other materials in a waste container.

3. Tools can be very dangerous. Never play with them. They are only meant to help you with your work.

4. Always be as careful as you can. Don't worry if you're slow. Remember that you are learning to be a housebuilder and that a house that is well-made is always better than a house someone has just slapped together.

Chapter 3

Using Your Tools

This chapter is written and illustrated to teach you how to use tools. Take these pages along with your tools and some scraps of soft wood to your workshop. Practice with each tool as shown in the following directions. Drive and pull 100 or more nails until you do it well. Saw 100 cuts or more until you saw straight. Keep working and learning the tools until you feel confident with each one. When you're ready, go on to Chapter Four and build the practice projects.

1. The Hammer

You'll be using the hammer just for driving and pulling nails. To drive a nail, it's important to tap it a few times to give it a start so that you don't have to hold it. Then you can hit the nail harder. Remember, it isn't important how many times you hit the nail to drive it all the way. It *is* important how straight it goes. Take your time and swing the hammer accurately.

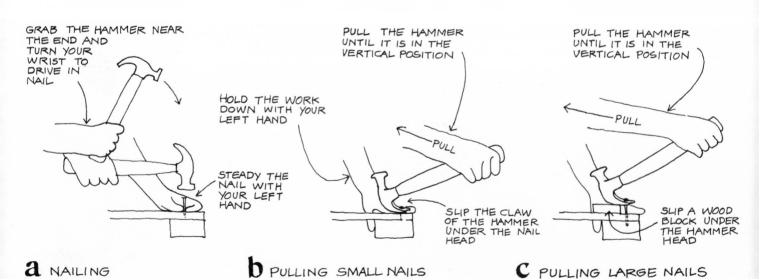

GRAB THE HAMMER NEAR THE END AND TURN YOUR WRIST TO DRIVE IN NAIL

STEADY THE NAIL WITH YOUR LEFT HAND

a NAILING

HOLD THE WORK DOWN WITH YOUR LEFT HAND

PULL THE HAMMER UNTIL IT IS IN THE VERTICAL POSITION

PULL

SLIP THE CLAW OF THE HAMMER UNDER THE NAIL HEAD

b PULLING SMALL NAILS

PULL THE HAMMER UNTIL IT IS IN THE VERTICAL POSITION

PULL

SLIP A WOOD BLOCK UNDER THE HAMMER HEAD

c PULLING LARGE NAILS

2. The Crosscut Saw

After you've drawn a pencil line showing where you want to saw, you're ready to start. Grasp the handle of the saw firmly in your right hand and draw, or pull, the saw up several times with the thumb of the left hand guiding the blade on the wood where the saw cut is to be made. Doing this will make a small groove in the wood that will keep the saw blade in place so that you can begin to saw along the pencil line. At the end of the cut, take short sawing strokes and hold the waste piece so that it doesn't break off and splinter. The saw is your most dangerous tool. Begin slowly and practice as much as you can.

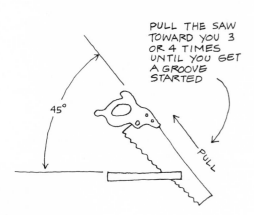

PULL THE SAW TOWARD YOU 3 OR 4 TIMES UNTIL YOU GET A GROOVE STARTED

45°

PULL

a SAW AT 45°

CAREFULLY SAW ALONG THE PENCIL LINE YOU HAVE DRAWN

TOUCH YOUR LEFT THUMB TO THE SAW AND LET THE SAW REST AGAINST IT UNTIL YOU GET THE GROOVE STARTED

b USE YOUR THUMB AS A GUIDE

USE YOUR KNEE TO HOLD THE WOOD DOWN TO THE TABLE

WORKBENCH

c SAWING SMALL PIECES

ASK A FRIEND TO BE A WEIGHT TO HOLD LARGE PIECES OF WOOD STEADY FOR YOU

ORANGE CRATES CAN BE USED FOR SAWING

d SAWING LARGE PIECES

3. The Level

The level is the tool that tells you when a wall is exactly vertical (plumb) or when a floor is exactly horizontal (level). The level has two slightly curved glass tubes, both filled with a liquid and a bubble of air. When the bubble floats to the center of the tube, between the two marks, it means that the level is either exactly vertical or horizontal. Later, as you build your house, you'll use the level to make sure your walls and floors aren't crooked.

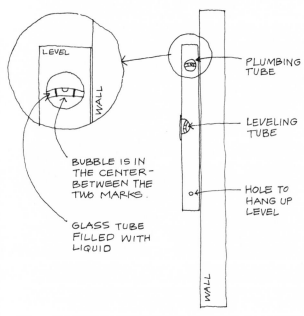

LEVEL

WALL

BUBBLE IS IN
THE CENTER-
BETWEEN THE
TWO MARKS.

GLASS TUBE
FILLED WITH
LIQUID

PLUMBING
TUBE

LEVELING
TUBE

HOLE TO
HANG UP
LEVEL

WALL

a A PLUMB (VERTICAL) WALL

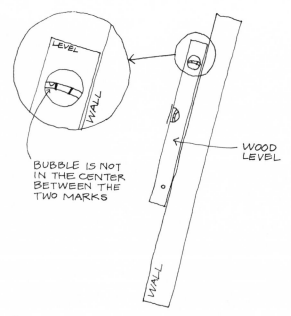

LEVEL

WALL

BUBBLE IS NOT
IN THE CENTER
BETWEEN THE
TWO MARKS

WOOD
LEVEL

WALL

b AN OUT-OF-PLUMB WALL

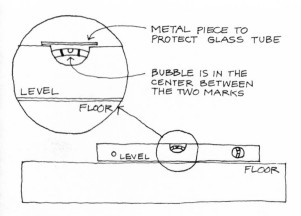

METAL PIECE TO
PROTECT GLASS TUBE

BUBBLE IS IN THE
CENTER BETWEEN
THE TWO MARKS

LEVEL

FLOOR

O LEVEL

FLOOR

c A LEVEL (HORIZONTAL) FLOOR

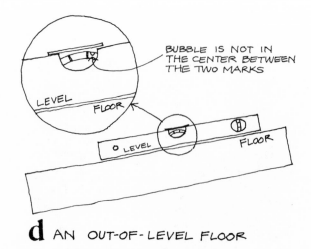

BUBBLE IS NOT IN
THE CENTER BETWEEN
THE TWO MARKS

LEVEL

FLOOR

O LEVEL

FLOOR

d AN OUT-OF-LEVEL FLOOR

4. The Keyhole Saw

This saw is primarily used to cut out windows and doors from the siding of your house. This is done by drilling a hole in the siding and then sliding the thin keyhole saw blade into the hole to saw out the window or door shape. The keyhole saw is also used to cut fancy shapes from wood that you can use as decoration on your house.

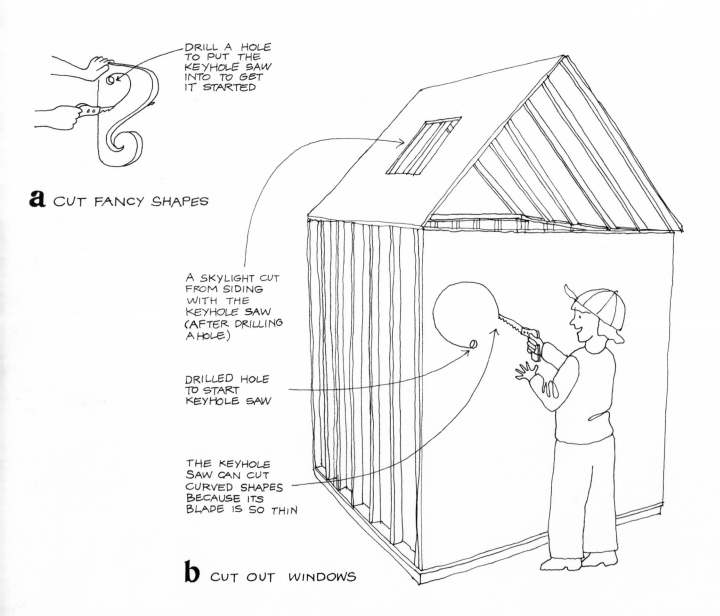

DRILL A HOLE TO PUT THE KEYHOLE SAW INTO TO GET IT STARTED

a CUT FANCY SHAPES

A SKYLIGHT CUT FROM SIDING WITH THE KEYHOLE SAW (AFTER DRILLING A HOLE)

DRILLED HOLE TO START KEYHOLE SAW

THE KEYHOLE SAW CAN CUT CURVED SHAPES BECAUSE ITS BLADE IS SO THIN

b CUT OUT WINDOWS

5. The Brace & Bit

You'll face three problems in drilling holes. The first problem is to drill straight. Solve this by asking a friend to stand back and line you up as you drill. The second problem is to drill without breaking through the wood at the bottom of the hole. Solve this by drilling through the wood until the point of the bit sticks out the other side (drawing B); then turn the wood over, put the point of the bit in the small hole and drill again from the other side. The third problem is to drill without making a hole in your workbench or any other surface. Solve this by putting a piece of scrap wood under the wood you are drilling.

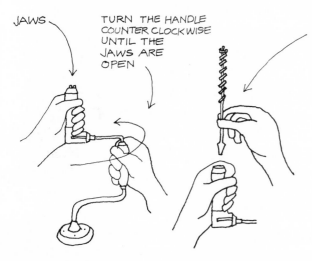

JAWS

TURN THE HANDLE COUNTER CLOCKWISE UNTIL THE JAWS ARE OPEN

PLACE THE DRILL BIT INTO THE JAWS AND TURN THE HANDLE CLOCKWISE UNTIL THE JAWS FIRMLY GRAB IT.

a PLACE THE BIT INTO THE BRACE

PLACE A PIECE OF SCRAP WOOD UNDER YOUR WORK OR DRILL OVER AN OPENING

TO HOLD THE WOOD STEADY NAIL IT TO YOUR WORKBENCH OR HAVE A FRIEND HOLD IT.

ORANGE CRATE

C DRILLING A VERTICAL HOLE

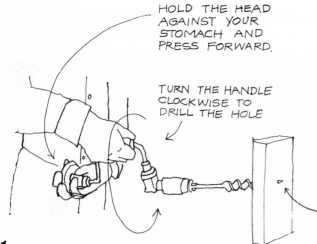

HOLD THE HEAD AGAINST YOUR STOMACH AND PRESS FORWARD.

TURN THE HANDLE CLOCKWISE TO DRILL THE HOLE

b DRILLING A HORIZONTAL HOLE

TO GET A PERFECT HOLE, DRILL THROUGH THE WOOD UNTIL THE POINT OF THE DRILL IS SHOWING. THEN REMOVE THE BIT FROM THE HOLE AND DRILL FROM THE OTHER SIDE, USING THE LITTLE HOLE TO START THE BIT AGAIN.

6. The Square

You'll be using the square, known as the "try square," to draw a perfectly straight line for sawing. When you use the square, press the handle hard against the edge of the wood, then draw a pencil line along the steel edge. You're now ready to make a perfect saw cut.

PRESS THE HANDLE HARD AGAINST THE EDGE OF THE WOOD

WOOD

yes

NOT ENOUGH PRESSURE ON THE HANDLE

WOOD

no

a PRESS THE TRY SQUARE AGAINST THE EDGE OF THE WOOD

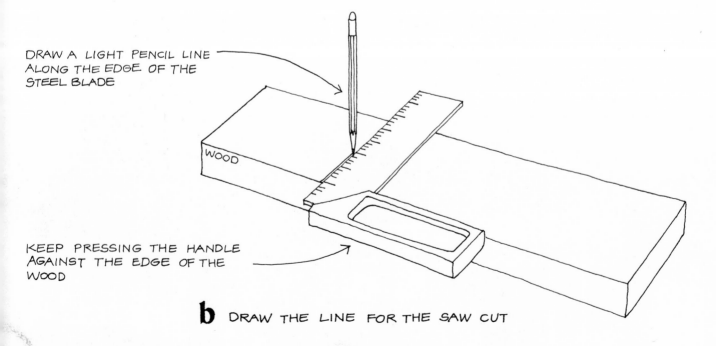

DRAW A LIGHT PENCIL LINE ALONG THE EDGE OF THE STEEL BLADE

WOOD

KEEP PRESSING THE HANDLE AGAINST THE EDGE OF THE WOOD

b DRAW THE LINE FOR THE SAW CUT

7. The Tape

The eight-foot steel measuring tape is a marked coil of tape that unrolls to measure boards up to eight feet long. You can use the tape by yourself by catching the hook on the edge of the board and pulling the cover away from that edge. Or have a friend help by holding one end of the tape. Measure the feet first, then the inches, and then the parts of inches. For example, if you must measure 1'-6½'' (' is the symbol for feet and '' is the symbol for inches) first find the 1' mark, then move along the tape until you find the 6'' mark, then move further along to the first ½'' mark.

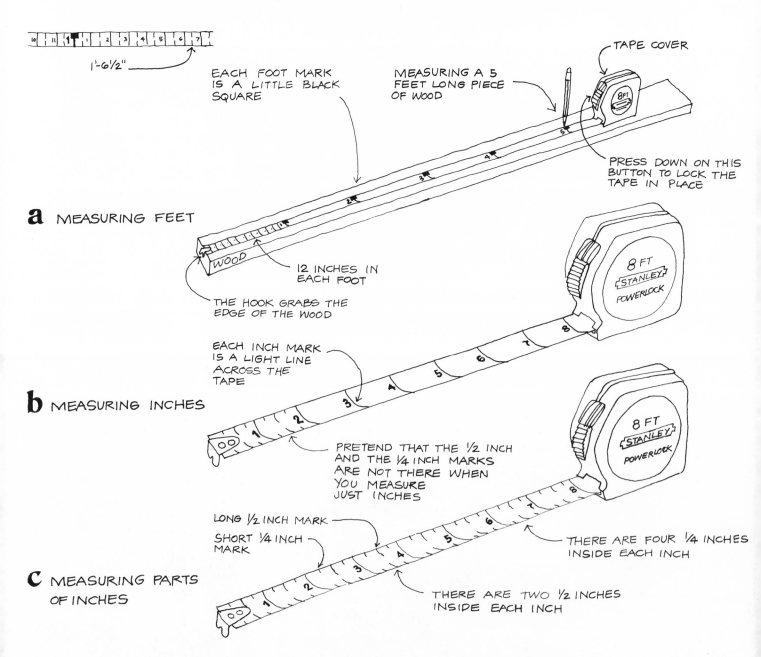

1'-6½''

TAPE COVER

EACH FOOT MARK IS A LITTLE BLACK SQUARE

MEASURING A 5 FEET LONG PIECE OF WOOD

PRESS DOWN ON THIS BUTTON TO LOCK THE TAPE IN PLACE

a MEASURING FEET

WOOD

12 INCHES IN EACH FOOT

THE HOOK GRABS THE EDGE OF THE WOOD

8 FT
STANLEY
POWERLOCK

EACH INCH MARK IS A LIGHT LINE ACROSS THE TAPE

b MEASURING INCHES

PRETEND THAT THE ½ INCH AND THE ¼ INCH MARKS ARE NOT THERE WHEN YOU MEASURE JUST INCHES

8 FT
STANLEY
POWERLOCK

LONG ½ INCH MARK

SHORT ¼ INCH MARK

THERE ARE FOUR ¼ INCHES INSIDE EACH INCH

c MEASURING PARTS OF INCHES

THERE ARE TWO ½ INCHES INSIDE EACH INCH

Chapter 4
Practice Projects

This chapter contains three projects to build after you've learned how to use all your tools. They're a test of your skills. If you can build all three and they are straight and sturdy, you're ready to build your house.

Remember to be careful and to take your time. If you hurry, you'll make mistakes that take time to correct. Drive your nails true and saw straight. Do your best work.

A Picture Frame

This project is the easiest of the three but you'll find that you must make perfect saw cuts and you must hammer your nails straight because all the parts should fit together well.

Read the step-by-step directions a few times, making sure you understand them before you start. You'll gain good experience for building the woodframe and the factory-built houses by completing this project. And the picture frame makes a nice present to give someone!

Step 1: Assembling the Tools & Materials

Here's a list of the tools and materials you'll need to build the picture frame. It's best to gather all of them in your workshop before you begin.

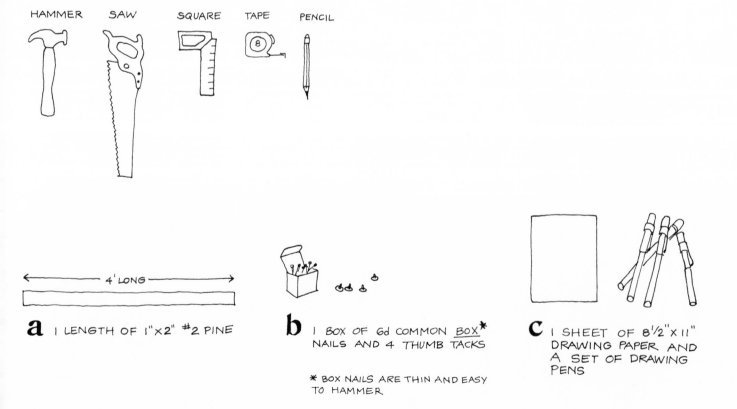

HAMMER   SAW   SQUARE   TAPE   PENCIL

a | LENGTH OF 1"x 2" #2 PINE — 4' LONG

b | BOX OF 6d COMMON <u>BOX</u>* NAILS AND 4 THUMB TACKS

* BOX NAILS ARE THIN AND EASY TO HAMMER

c | SHEET OF 8½"x 11" DRAWING PAPER AND A SET OF DRAWING PENS

Step 2: Laying Out the Parts

Here are the directions to follow to lay out the parts for the picture frame. Be careful to measure the correct lengths along the wood piece and to mark the names of each piece before sawing (side, top, bottom).

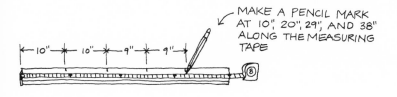

MAKE A PENCIL MARK AT 10", 20", 29", AND 38" ALONG THE MEASURING TAPE

a MEASURE THE TOP, BOTTOM AND SIDE PIECES

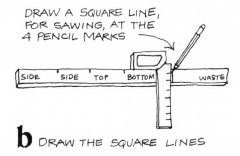

DRAW A SQUARE LINE, FOR SAWING, AT THE 4 PENCIL MARKS

b DRAW THE SQUARE LINES

Step 3: Sawing the Parts

Here are the directions for sawing your frame parts. If you own a drawing or painting that you would like to frame, you can trim it to 8½" by 11".

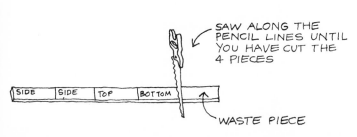

SAW ALONG THE PENCIL LINES UNTIL YOU HAVE CUT THE 4 PIECES

WASTE PIECE

a CUT THE TOP, BOTTOM AND SIDE PIECES

b MAKE ANY DRAWING THAT YOU LIKE

Step 4: Assembling the Parts

After you've done all your sawing, you're ready to nail the parts together. Just follow the instructions below, remembering that when one of your nails starts to go crooked, pull it out and start again.

If you like, you can use two of the nails to attach a wire to the back of the frame for hanging.

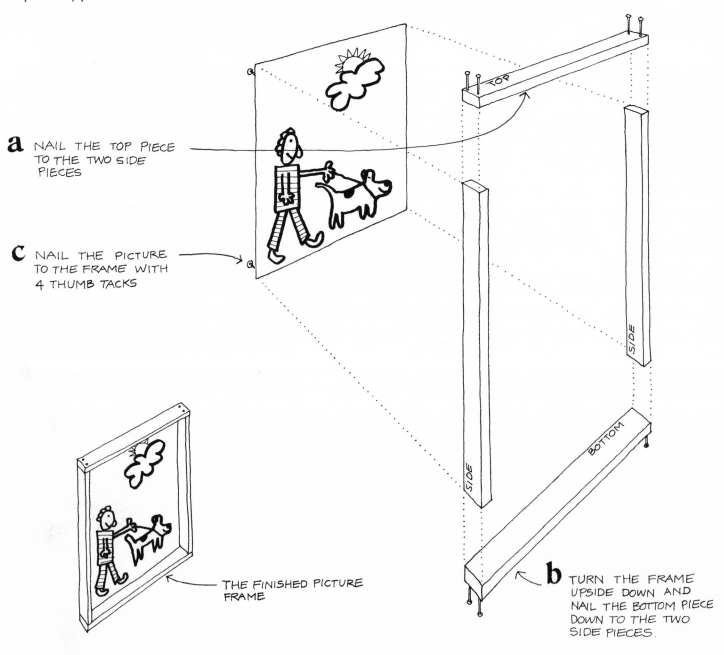

a NAIL THE TOP PIECE TO THE TWO SIDE PIECES

c NAIL THE PICTURE TO THE FRAME WITH 4 THUMB TACKS

TOP

SIDE

SIDE

BOTTOM

THE FINISHED PICTURE FRAME

b TURN THE FRAME UPSIDE DOWN AND NAIL THE BOTTOM PIECE DOWN TO THE TWO SIDE PIECES.

A Tool Box

Here's a project that you really need and should build for yourself. Later, you'll want and need to carry your tools from your outdoor workshop to your house.

Remember to read the complete instructions until you understand them. Be as neat and careful as you can. After all, what's a housebuilder without a beautiful well-built tool box?

Step 1: Assembling the Tools & Materials

Here's a list of tools and materials to gather in your workshop.

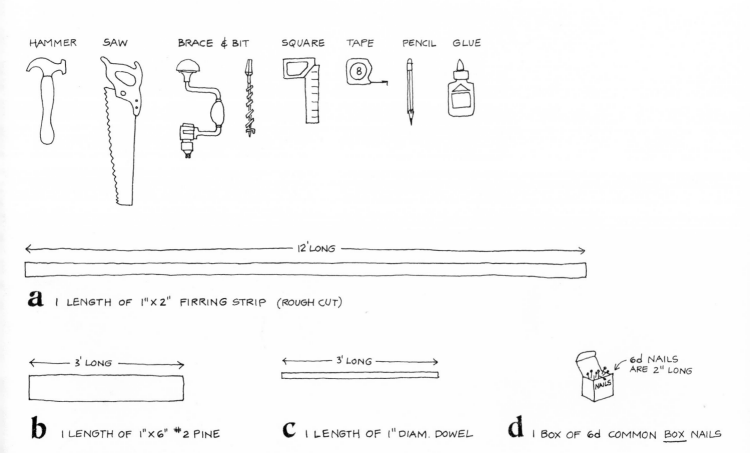

HAMMER   SAW   BRACE & BIT   SQUARE   TAPE   PENCIL   GLUE

a 1 LENGTH OF 1"X 2" FIRRING STRIP (ROUGH CUT) — 12' LONG

b 1 LENGTH OF 1"X6" #2 PINE — 3' LONG

c 1 LENGTH OF 1" DIAM. DOWEL — 3' LONG

d 1 BOX OF 6d COMMON BOX NAILS — 6d NAILS ARE 2" LONG

Step 2: Laying Out the Parts

Here are the instructions to follow to lay out the tool box parts.

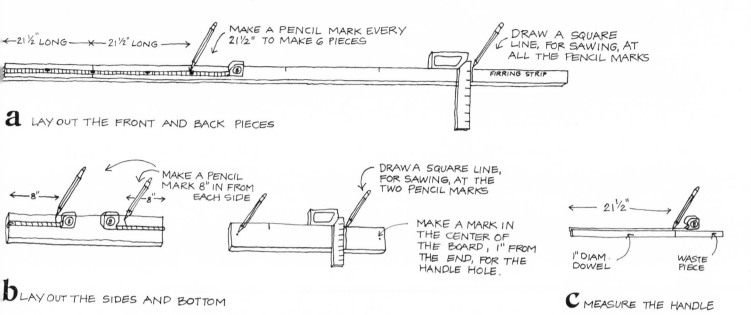

←—21½" LONG—→×—21½" LONG—→   MAKE A PENCIL MARK EVERY 21½" TO MAKE 6 PIECES   DRAW A SQUARE LINE, FOR SAWING, AT ALL THE PENCIL MARKS

FIRRING STRIP

a LAY OUT THE FRONT AND BACK PIECES

←8"→ ←8"→   MAKE A PENCIL MARK 8" IN FROM EACH SIDE

DRAW A SQUARE LINE, FOR SAWING, AT THE TWO PENCIL MARKS

MAKE A MARK IN THE CENTER OF THE BOARD, 1" FROM THE END, FOR THE HANDLE HOLE.

←—21½"—→

1" DIAM. DOWEL   WASTE PIECE

b LAY OUT THE SIDES AND BOTTOM

c MEASURE THE HANDLE

Step 3: Sawing the Parts

Here are the instructions for sawing and drilling all the parts.

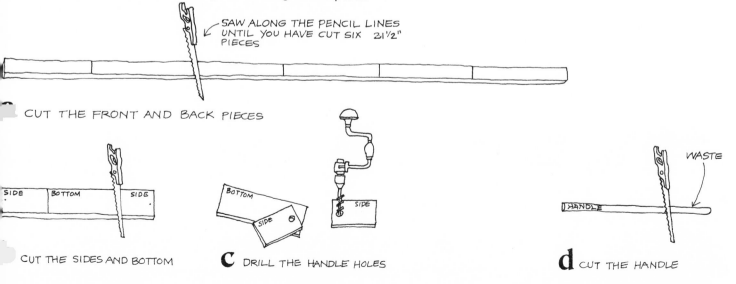

SAW ALONG THE PENCIL LINES UNTIL YOU HAVE CUT SIX 21½" PIECES

CUT THE FRONT AND BACK PIECES

SIDE   BOTTOM   SIDE

CUT THE SIDES AND BOTTOM

BOTTOM   SIDE   SIDE

c DRILL THE HANDLE HOLES

WASTE

HANDLE

d CUT THE HANDLE

Step 4: Assembling the Parts

Before you nail your tool box together, hold the parts against each other to make sure they fit well. It's easy to fix a mistake before the pieces are nailed together.

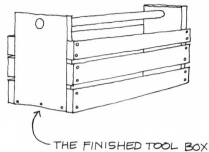

THE FINISHED TOOL BOX

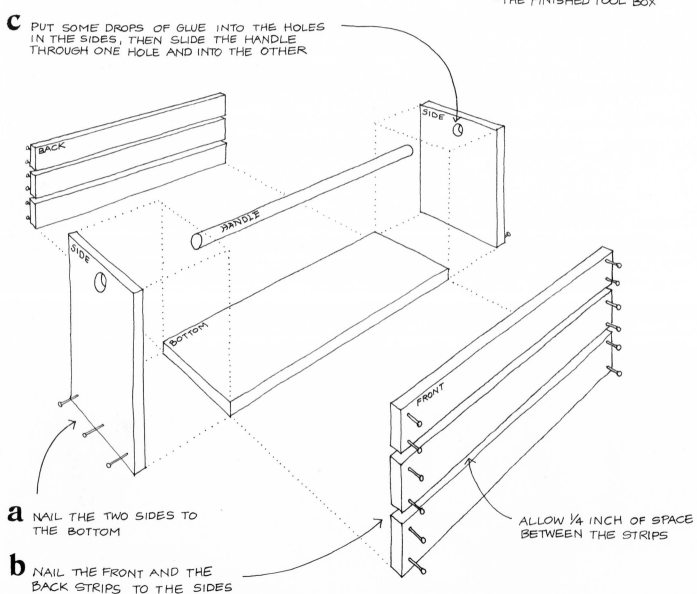

c PUT SOME DROPS OF GLUE INTO THE HOLES IN THE SIDES, THEN SLIDE THE HANDLE THROUGH ONE HOLE AND INTO THE OTHER

BACK

SIDE

HANDLE

SIDE

BOTTOM

FRONT

ALLOW ¼ INCH OF SPACE BETWEEN THE STRIPS

a NAIL THE TWO SIDES TO THE BOTTOM

b NAIL THE FRONT AND THE BACK STRIPS TO THE SIDES

46

A Tugboat

Here's a simple project you can use in the nearest stream or as a present for a friend who likes to take baths. You might want to make two or three tugboats after you find how easy they are to build.

Remember to work very carefully. Don't ever hammer a crooked nail. You're teaching yourself to be a good carpenter.

Step 1: Assembling the Tools & Materials

Here's a list of tools and materials to gather in your workshop.

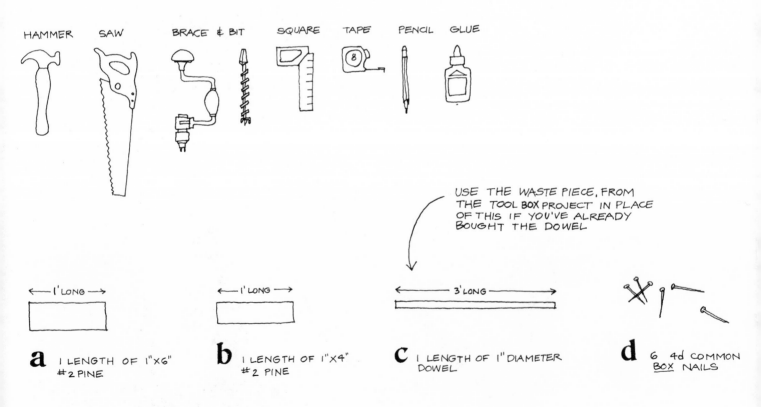

HAMMER   SAW   BRACE & BIT   SQUARE   TAPE   PENCIL   GLUE

USE THE WASTE PIECE, FROM THE TOOL BOX PROJECT IN PLACE OF THIS IF YOU'VE ALREADY BOUGHT THE DOWEL

a 1 LENGTH OF 1"x6" #2 PINE
← 1' LONG →

b 1 LENGTH OF 1"x4" #2 PINE
← 1' LONG →

c 1 LENGTH OF 1" DIAMETER DOWEL
← 3' LONG →

d 6 4d COMMON BOX NAILS

Step 2: Laying Out the Parts

Here are the directions to lay out the tugboat's parts.

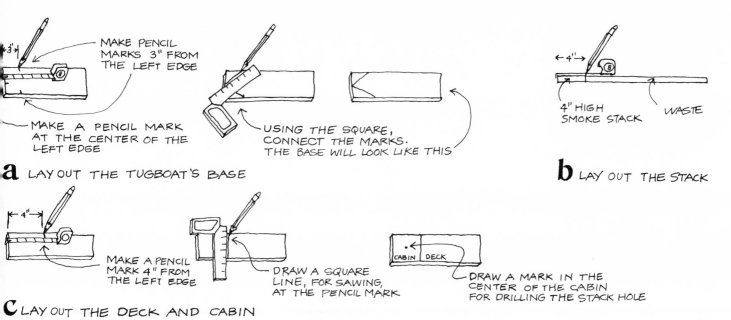

a LAY OUT THE TUGBOAT'S BASE

MAKE PENCIL MARKS 3" FROM THE LEFT EDGE

MAKE A PENCIL MARK AT THE CENTER OF THE LEFT EDGE

USING THE SQUARE, CONNECT THE MARKS. THE BASE WILL LOOK LIKE THIS

b LAY OUT THE STACK

4" HIGH SMOKE STACK

WASTE

c LAY OUT THE DECK AND CABIN

MAKE A PENCIL MARK 4" FROM THE LEFT EDGE

DRAW A SQUARE LINE, FOR SAWING, AT THE PENCIL MARK

CABIN DECK

DRAW A MARK IN THE CENTER OF THE CABIN FOR DRILLING THE STACK HOLE

Step 3: Sawing the Parts

Here are directions to saw and drill all the parts you'll need.

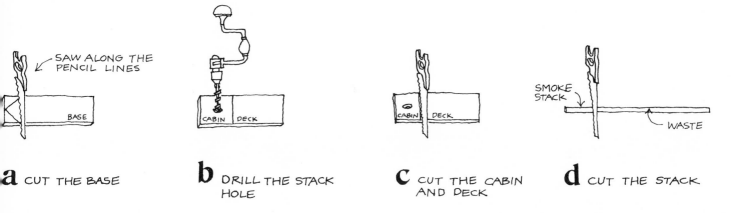

a CUT THE BASE

SAW ALONG THE PENCIL LINES

BASE

b DRILL THE STACK HOLE

CABIN DECK

c CUT THE CABIN AND DECK

CABIN DECK

d CUT THE STACK

SMOKE STACK

WASTE

Step 4: Assembling the Parts

Here are the instructions to follow in assembling your tugboat. You might want to paint the smoke stack or the other parts before you nail or glue them together.

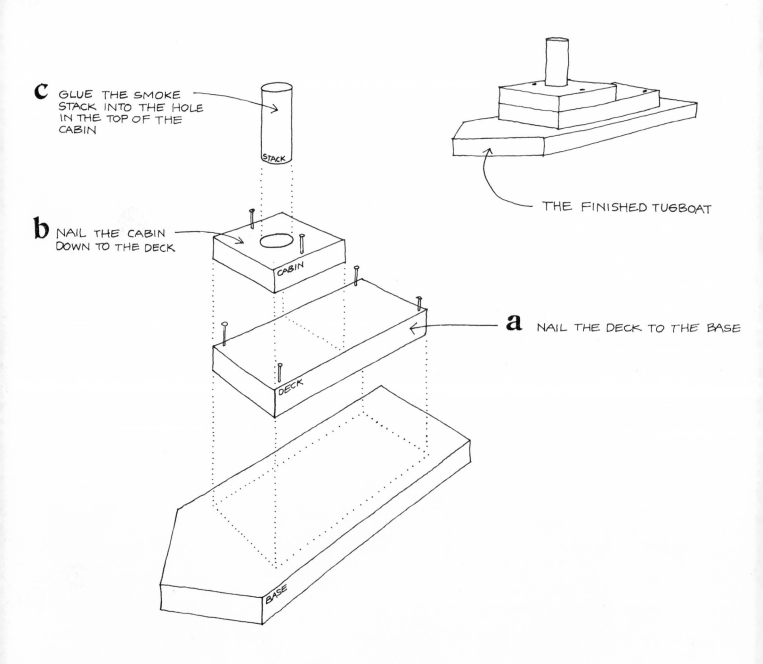

c GLUE THE SMOKE STACK INTO THE HOLE IN THE TOP OF THE CABIN

STACK

b NAIL THE CABIN DOWN TO THE DECK

CABIN

a NAIL THE DECK TO THE BASE

DECK

BASE

THE FINISHED TUGBOAT

Chapter 5

6 Houses To Build

Now that you've learned how to use all of your tools, you're ready to build your house.

First, of course, choose which house you like from those six pictured on the next page. To do this become very familiar with the houses by studying Chapter Five. While studying, try to keep in mind what you'll do in your house after it's finished. If it's just to be used as a playhouse, you may choose the woodframe, the post and beam, or the junkyard houses. If you want a house that's warm early in the spring in a cold climate (where you can grow plants) you might prefer the glass house. If you live where there are big trees you might want the tree house. And if you want a house that you can change into a fort, you may want to choose the factory-built house. Make sure you choose the house that's right for you.

Next, choose your site, the place to build your house. Talk with your parents or teacher about this. You'll want to pick a spot that will make everybody happy. Remember that you'll need at least a 15' by 20' area, cleared and flat, to store your materials and to use for building space. The glass house will need direct sunlight if it is to be warm.

Choose A House

The Woodframe House

The Factory-built House

The Glass House

The Post and Beam House

The Junkyard House

The Tree House

The Woodframe House

For the last one hundred years most of the houses in America have been built around a wood frame made from many thin pieces of wood. This way of building a house is now known as the "balloon frame" because it's so light.

Since the invention of the balloon frame it has been possible for one carpenter, working alone, to build an entire house. This was impossible earlier because the wooden beams and columns used to build early American houses were so heavy. An excellent reference book about building a large woodframe house is *Illustrated Housebuilding* by Graham Blackburn (see the Appendix).

If you plan to be a housebuilder when you get older, this is the house for you. Our woodframe house is built exactly like the modern balloon frame house you see around your neighborhood. You'll learn how to build a wall on the ground and tilt it up into place. You'll find out how to frame windows and doors. And you'll see how to build a strong roof.

This house may look difficult to build but if you take one step at a time, you'll see how easy it is.

SO WHEN DO WE MOVE IN, HAROLD?

Step 1
Assembling the Tools

A good housebuilder always gets the tools needed for work ready before starting. This way work never gets interrupted. Try to get the habit. Carefully assemble the tools listed below on your workbench. Make sure they're all working well.

1 HAMMER
FOR NAILING

4 KEYHOLE SAW
FOR CUTTING OUT WINDOWS &
SKYLIGHTS IN SIDING & ROOFING

7 TAPE
FOR MEASURING A
MATERIAL TO THE
RIGHT SIZE

2 CROSS CUT SAW
FOR CUTTING THE WOOD PIECES
TO THE RIGHT LENGTH

5 BRACE & BIT
FOR DRILLING HOLES
IN THE SIDING & ROOFING
TO GET THE KEYHOLE SAW
STARTED

8 BANDAGES
FOR CUTS

3 LEVEL
FOR LEVELING THE BASE SO
THAT THE HOUSE IS STRAIGHT

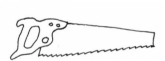

6 SQUARE
FOR MARKING A
PERPENDICULAR LINE
ON WOOD THAT IS TO
BE SAWED

9 CARPENTER'S
APRON
TO HOLD NAILS &
HAMMER

Step 2
Assembling the Materials

Here's a list of materials needed to build the woodframe house. You should be able to order them all and have them delivered from the lumber yard.

Make sure the Homosote sheets are sawn in half as shown below. Lumber yards will usually do this at no charge and it will save you some rather difficult work.

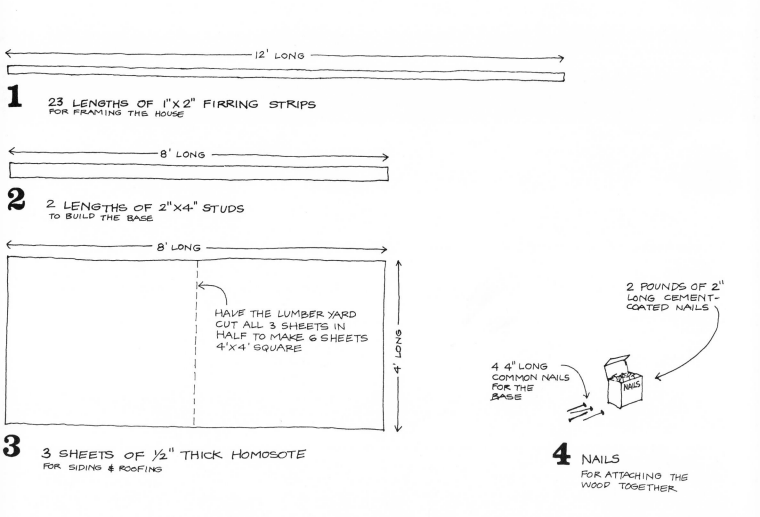

← 12' LONG →

1 23 LENGTHS OF 1"X 2" FIRRING STRIPS
FOR FRAMING THE HOUSE

← 8' LONG →

2 2 LENGTHS OF 2"X4" STUDS
TO BUILD THE BASE

← 8' LONG →

HAVE THE LUMBER YARD CUT ALL 3 SHEETS IN HALF TO MAKE 6 SHEETS 4'X4' SQUARE

4' LONG

3 3 SHEETS OF 1/2" THICK HOMOSOTE
FOR SIDING & ROOFING

2 POUNDS OF 2" LONG CEMENT-COATED NAILS

4 4" LONG COMMON NAILS FOR THE BASE

4 NAILS
FOR ATTACHING THE WOOD TOGETHER

Step 3
Measuring and Sawing the Wall Pieces

In order to build the four walls of the house, you'll need thirty-six 4'-long lengths of firring strips. To make these, divide twelve 12' lengths of firring strips, each into three equal pieces. This will give you thirty-six 4'-long pieces. The instructions for measuring and sawing one of these 12'-long lengths are given below. Follow the same instructions for eleven more of the 12' lengths.

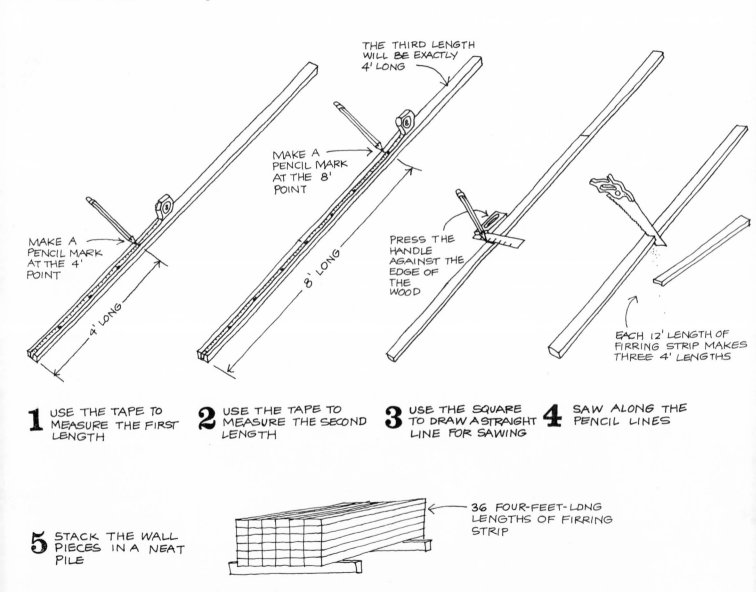

THE THIRD LENGTH WILL BE EXACTLY 4' LONG

MAKE A PENCIL MARK AT THE 8' POINT

MAKE A PENCIL MARK AT THE 4' POINT

4' LONG

8' LONG

PRESS THE HANDLE AGAINST THE EDGE OF THE WOOD

EACH 12' LENGTH OF FIRRING STRIP MAKES THREE 4' LENGTHS

1 USE THE TAPE TO MEASURE THE FIRST LENGTH

2 USE THE TAPE TO MEASURE THE SECOND LENGTH

3 USE THE SQUARE TO DRAW A STRAIGHT LINE FOR SAWING

4 SAW ALONG THE PENCIL LINES

5 STACK THE WALL PIECES IN A NEAT PILE

36 FOUR-FEET-LONG LENGTHS OF FIRRING STRIP

Step 4
Building the Four Walls

Take nine of the firring strips you've just cut into 4' lengths. Make one a top piece, one a bottom piece, and seven of them wall pieces. We call the wall pieces "studs." Make pencil marks 8" apart along the top and bottom pieces, then nail them together as shown in the drawing below.

Follow these directions three more times and you'll have built four identical walls.

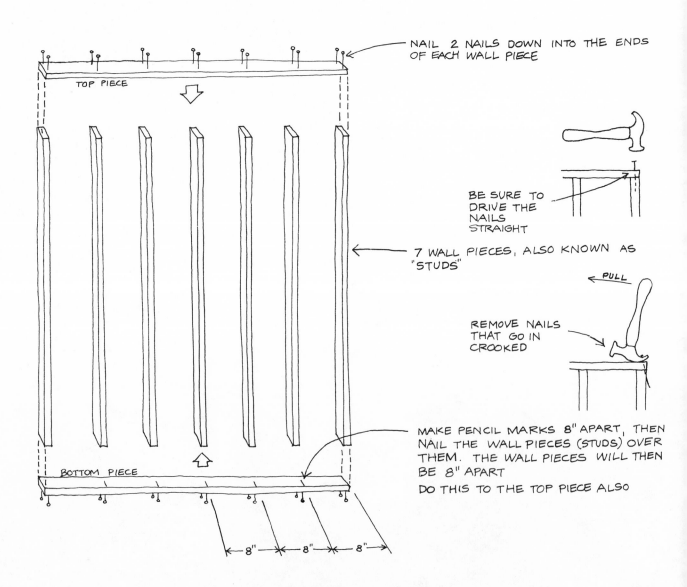

NAIL 2 NAILS DOWN INTO THE ENDS OF EACH WALL PIECE

TOP PIECE

BE SURE TO DRIVE THE NAILS STRAIGHT

7 WALL PIECES, ALSO KNOWN AS "STUDS"

PULL

REMOVE NAILS THAT GO IN CROOKED

MAKE PENCIL MARKS 8" APART, THEN NAIL THE WALL PIECES (STUDS) OVER THEM. THE WALL PIECES WILL THEN BE 8" APART
DO THIS TO THE TOP PIECE ALSO

BOTTOM PIECE

8"   8"   8"

Step 5
Building the Base

Saw the two 8' long 2"x4" studs into 4 pieces. Then nail them together to make the square base shown below.

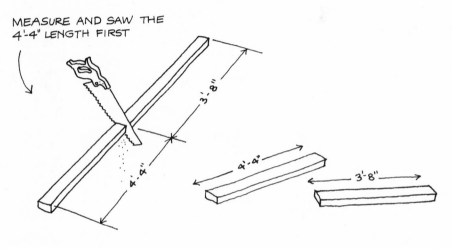

MEASURE AND SAW THE
4'-4" LENGTH FIRST

3'-8"

4'-4"

3'-8"

1 SAW EACH 8' LONG
2"x4" INTO 2 PIECES

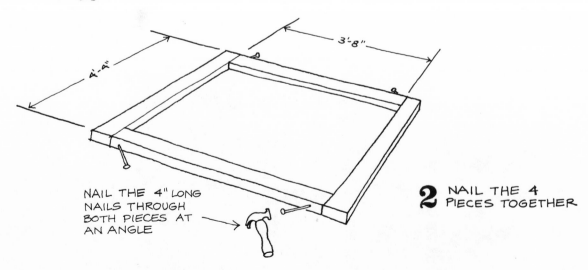

3'-8"

4'-4"

NAIL THE 4" LONG
NAILS THROUGH
BOTH PIECES AT
AN ANGLE

2 NAIL THE 4
PIECES TOGETHER

Step 6
Attaching the Walls to the Base

Now you're ready to tilt your woodframe walls into place. Ask a friend to hold the first wall as you line it up over the base. Now drive in the first nail.

It's important to drive the first few nails in just half-way, until you're sure that the walls all line up with one another. After you're sure, drive the nails in all the way. Make sure that the nails at the corners are in straight to add to the strength of the house.

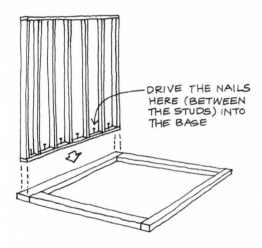

DRIVE THE NAILS HERE (BETWEEN THE STUDS) INTO THE BASE

1 NAIL THE FIRST WALL TO THE BASE

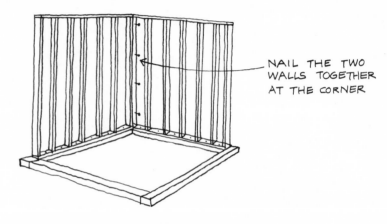

NAIL THE TWO WALLS TOGETHER AT THE CORNER

2 NAIL THE SECOND WALL TO THE BASE

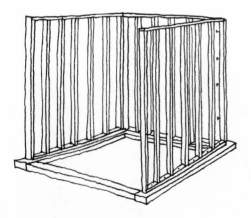

3 NAIL THE THIRD WALL TO THE BASE

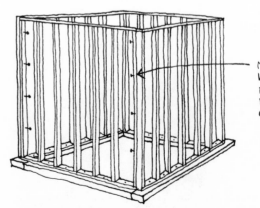

NAIL THE FOURTH WALL TO THE FIRST AND THIRD WALLS AT THE CORNERS

4 NAIL THE FOURTH WALL TO THE BASE

Step 7
Framing the Door

Once you've decided where you want the door, saw a stud away so that your door will be wide enough to walk through. Saw this stud off at the height you want your door. Next, strengthen the frame around the door by nailing firring strips to the frame.

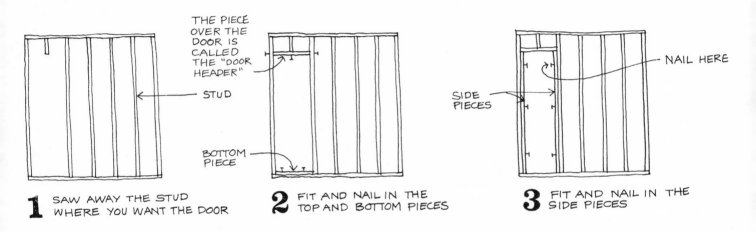

THE PIECE OVER THE DOOR IS CALLED THE "DOOR HEADER"

STUD

BOTTOM PIECE

SIDE PIECES

NAIL HERE

1 SAW AWAY THE STUD WHERE YOU WANT THE DOOR

2 FIT AND NAIL IN THE TOP AND BOTTOM PIECES

3 FIT AND NAIL IN THE SIDE PIECES

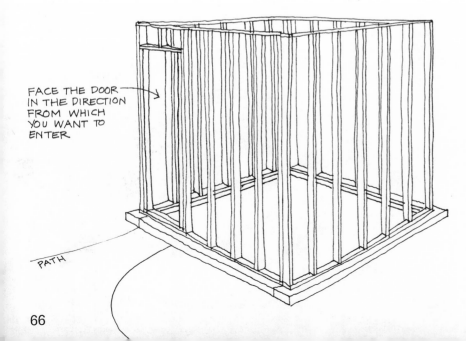

FACE THE DOOR IN THE DIRECTION FROM WHICH YOU WANT TO ENTER

PATH

Step 8
Framing the Windows

After you've built the door, stand inside your house and look out through the four walls to decide where the windows will go. You may want to make a picture window in the wall with the best view. Or you may want to make a little window in the wall facing the path to see who's coming. Or you may want to place a window in the direction of the wind to keep your house cool in the summer. Note where the sun enters your house. Then build windows that let in the sun's rays, if you want a sunny room.

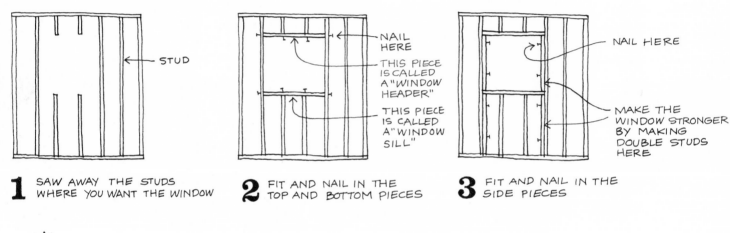

← STUD

NAIL HERE

THIS PIECE IS CALLED A "WINDOW HEADER"

THIS PIECE IS CALLED A "WINDOW SILL"

NAIL HERE

MAKE THE WINDOW STRONGER BY MAKING DOUBLE STUDS HERE

1 SAW AWAY THE STUDS WHERE YOU WANT THE WINDOW

2 FIT AND NAIL IN THE TOP AND BOTTOM PIECES

3 FIT AND NAIL IN THE SIDE PIECES

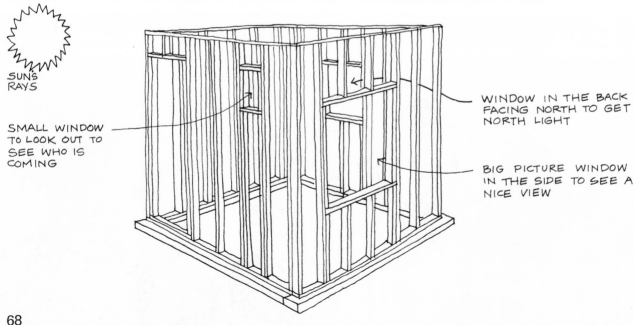

SUN'S RAYS

SMALL WINDOW TO LOOK OUT TO SEE WHO IS COMING

WINDOW IN THE BACK FACING NORTH TO GET NORTH LIGHT

BIG PICTURE WINDOW IN THE SIDE TO SEE A NICE VIEW

Step 9
Measuring and Sawing the Roof Rafters

Roof rafters are a little hard to lay out and saw because they have angles. Take your time and make sure that your pencil lines are correct before you saw. It's best to get one rafter right; then use it as a pattern to trace for the remaining 13 rafters.

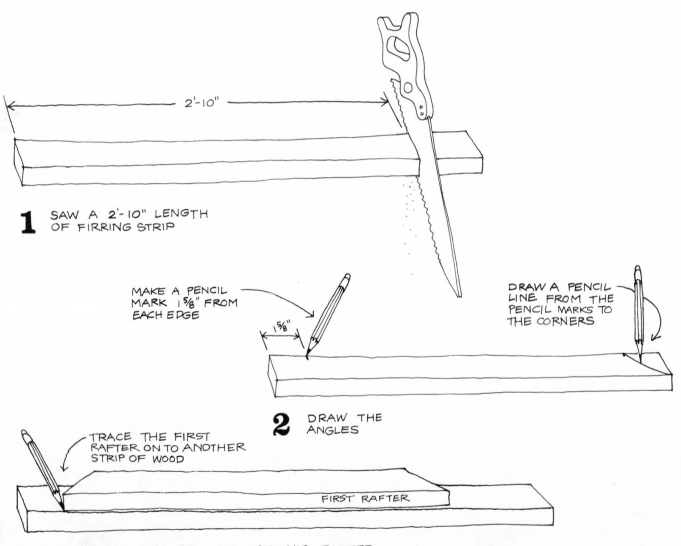

1 SAW A 2'-10" LENGTH OF FIRRING STRIP

MAKE A PENCIL MARK 1⅝" FROM EACH EDGE

DRAW A PENCIL LINE FROM THE PENCIL MARKS TO THE CORNERS

2 DRAW THE ANGLES

TRACE THE FIRST RAFTER ON TO ANOTHER STRIP OF WOOD

FIRST RAFTER

3 SAW THE ANGLES AND USE THIS RAFTER AS A PATTERN TO LAY OUT 13 MORE RAFTERS

REPEAT THESE STEPS UNTIL YOU HAVE MADE 14 RAFTERS.

Step 10
Framing the Roof

You'll need a small stepladder, placed inside the house, to stand high enough to nail the rafters in place. It's best to have a friend hand the rafters up to you and to hold them steady while you nail. Space the rafters 8″ apart by making pencil marks 8″ apart along the king post (the beam along the peak of the roof) and nailing the rafters over these marks.

Don't worry if the completed roof frame is a little shaky. It'll get strong when the roof is nailed down.

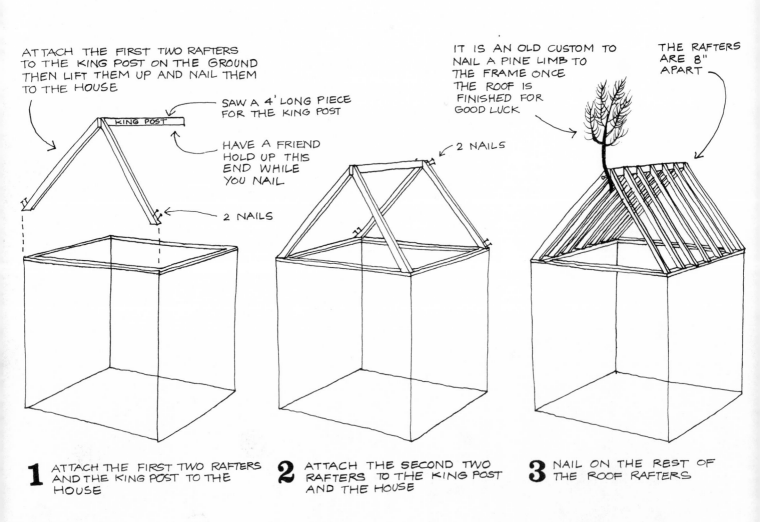

ATTACH THE FIRST TWO RAFTERS TO THE KING POST ON THE GROUND THEN LIFT THEM UP AND NAIL THEM TO THE HOUSE

KING POST

SAW A 4' LONG PIECE FOR THE KING POST

HAVE A FRIEND HOLD UP THIS END WHILE YOU NAIL

2 NAILS

IT IS AN OLD CUSTOM TO NAIL A PINE LIMB TO THE FRAME ONCE THE ROOF IS FINISHED FOR GOOD LUCK

2 NAILS

THE RAFTERS ARE 8″ APART

1 ATTACH THE FIRST TWO RAFTERS AND THE KING POST TO THE HOUSE

2 ATTACH THE SECOND TWO RAFTERS TO THE KING POST AND THE HOUSE

3 NAIL ON THE REST OF THE ROOF RAFTERS

Step 11
Attaching the Roofing and Siding

Now you're ready to install the roofing and siding to your frame. Take the 6 pieces of 4'x4' Homosote and nail them to the frame with the 2''-long nails. Start by nailing one of the sides around its edges into the frame. Then nail the next side, the front and the back into place. Trim the two roofing pieces from 4'x4' into 4'x2'-10'' by sawing off a 1'-2'' piece. Then nail them down into the roof rafters and the king post.

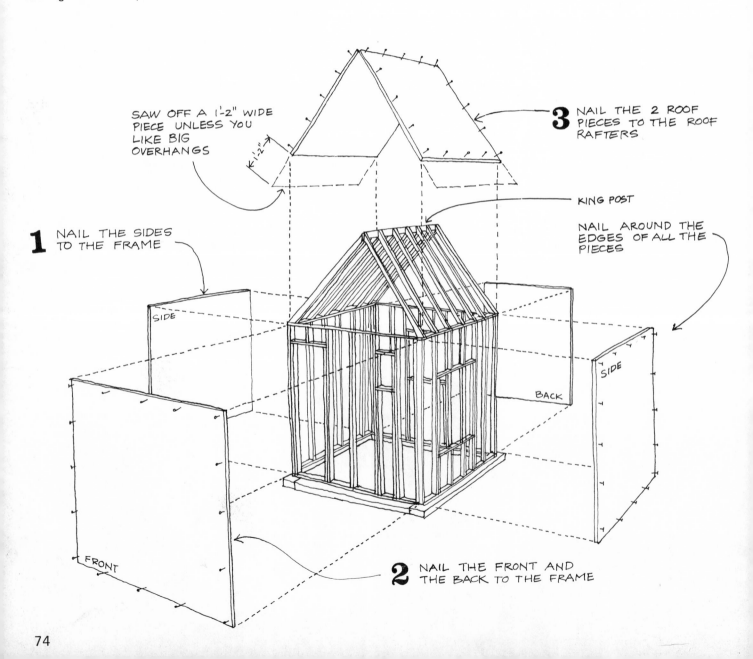

SAW OFF A 1'-2" WIDE PIECE UNLESS YOU LIKE BIG OVERHANGS

3 NAIL THE 2 ROOF PIECES TO THE ROOF RAFTERS

KING POST

NAIL AROUND THE EDGES OF ALL THE PIECES

1 NAIL THE SIDES TO THE FRAME

SIDE

SIDE

BACK

FRONT

2 NAIL THE FRONT AND THE BACK TO THE FRAME

Step 12
Sawing Out the Windows and Door

To put in your windows and doors, first drill a hole into the window and door openings (through the siding) to start the keyhole saw. Stick the point of the saw into the hole and saw around the edge of the window or door opening. It's easiest to do this from the inside because you can see the window and door frames. But you'll have to climb up your ladder and into the house through the opening below the roof. If you can't manage this, drill and saw by feel from the outside. If you feel yourself sawing the wood frame, you'll know you're off line.

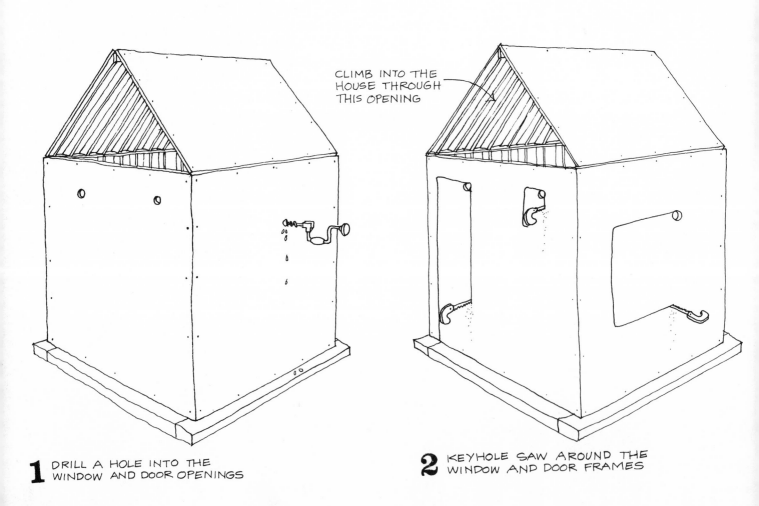

CLIMB INTO THE HOUSE THROUGH THIS OPENING

1 DRILL A HOLE INTO THE WINDOW AND DOOR OPENINGS

2 KEYHOLE SAW AROUND THE WINDOW AND DOOR FRAMES

Step 13
Nailing Around the Windows and Door

To finish your house you still have to nail the siding to the wood frame around the door and windows. This will make the house much stronger and will keep the siding from breaking away from the frame.

You're ready now for a huge house-warming party. Invite all your friends, your teachers and parents .... everyone!

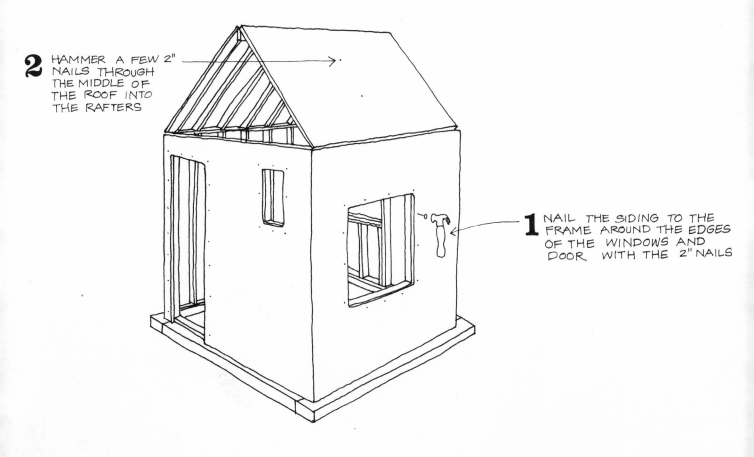

2 HAMMER A FEW 2" NAILS THROUGH THE MIDDLE OF THE ROOF INTO THE RAFTERS

1 NAIL THE SIDING TO THE FRAME AROUND THE EDGES OF THE WINDOWS AND DOOR WITH THE 2" NAILS

The Factory-built House

For the last fifty years, America has been developing easy to build houses in factories. These houses are built on an assembly line, just like cars, so that they can be assembled nearly anywhere very quickly and inexpensively. Trailers are still a popular kind of house built in a factory. A good book on this subject is *A History of Prefabrication* by Alfred Bruce and Harold Sandbank (see the Appendix).

Our house is meant to be built in a factory (we'll call it a workshop) and later delivered to the building site. The walls are panels that fit together and have windows and doors already cut out in your workshop. When the parts are delivered to the site, they can be erected in less than an hour.

Of course, if the weather's good, you can set up an outdoor "factory" next to your building site and eliminate the delivery problem.

Step 1
Assembling the Tools

Below is a list of the tools you'll need to build the factory-built house. Remember to assemble them on your workbench, checking to see that they all work well before you begin building.

The paint roller and tray may be new to you. You'll learn how to use them later in this chapter.

1 HAMMER
FOR NAILING

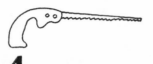

4 KEYHOLE SAW
FOR CUTTING OUT WINDOWS
AND DOORS IN THE PANELS

7 TAPE
FOR MEASURING A
MATERIAL

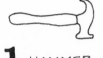

2 CROSSCUT SAW
FOR CUTTING THE
FIRRING STRIPS TO THE
RIGHT LENGTH

5 BRACE & BIT
FOR DRILLING HOLES IN
THE PANELS TO GET THE
KEYHOLE SAW STARTED AND
FOR DRILLING HOLES IN
THE CORNER POSTS

8 BANDAGES
FOR CUTS

3 PAINT ROLLER & TRAY
FOR PAINTING THE
PANELS

6 SQUARE
FOR MARKING A
STRAIGHT LINE
ON WOOD TO
BE SAWED

9 APRON
FOR HOLDING
NAILS

Step 2
Assembling the Materials

Below is the list of materials you'll need to build the largest of the factory-built houses shown on page 102. This house has 12 panels.

If you choose the smaller house — the one with just 4 panels — you'll only need 6 lengths of 1¼''x3'' firring strips, 2 lengths of 2''x3''s, 2 sheets of ¼'' plywood, two 1'' dowels, 1 quart of paint, and one pound of nails.

After you've made your list of materials, order them from your lumber yard and have them deliver everything to the site. Have your parents or teacher check it out to make sure you've received the correct amount of materials.

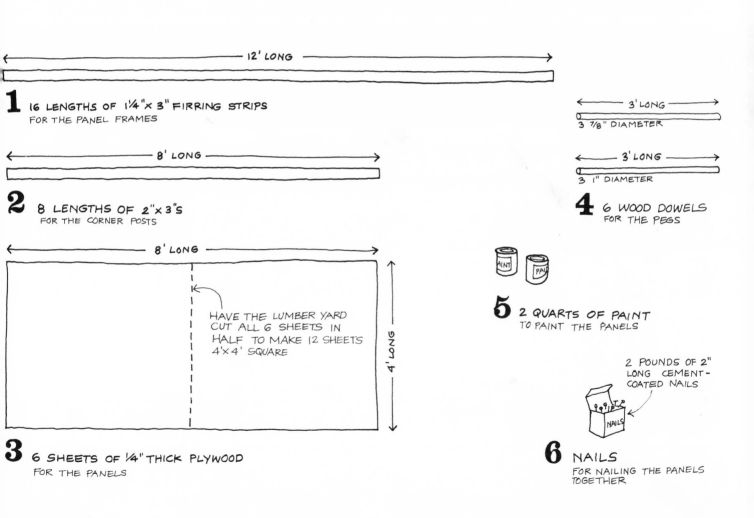

1 16 LENGTHS OF 1¼''x 3'' FIRRING STRIPS
FOR THE PANEL FRAMES
— 12' LONG —

2 8 LENGTHS OF 2''x3''s
FOR THE CORNER POSTS
— 8' LONG —

3 6 SHEETS OF ¼'' THICK PLYWOOD
FOR THE PANELS
— 8' LONG — 4' LONG —
HAVE THE LUMBER YARD CUT ALL 6 SHEETS IN HALF TO MAKE 12 SHEETS 4'x 4' SQUARE

4 6 WOOD DOWELS
FOR THE PEGS
— 3' LONG — 3 ⅞'' DIAMETER
— 3' LONG — 3 1'' DIAMETER

5 2 QUARTS OF PAINT
TO PAINT THE PANELS

6 NAILS
FOR NAILING THE PANELS TOGETHER
2 POUNDS OF 2'' LONG CEMENT-COATED NAILS

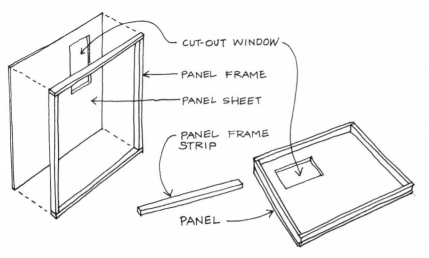

CUT-OUT WINDOW

PANEL FRAME

PANEL SHEET

PANEL FRAME STRIP

PANEL

Here's a drawing of one of the many similar panels you'll need to build for the walls of your factory-built house. The panel sheets are cut from 4'x4' plywood sheets. The panel strip is a piece of 1''x3'' firring strip and the frame is made from four panel strips.

Step 3
Measuring the Panel Frame Strips

Your first job is to measure 24 firring strips 4' long and 24 firring strips 3'-10'' long. These will be the 48 strips you need for the 12 panel frames. Remember: you can saw three lengths from one 12' length of firring strip.

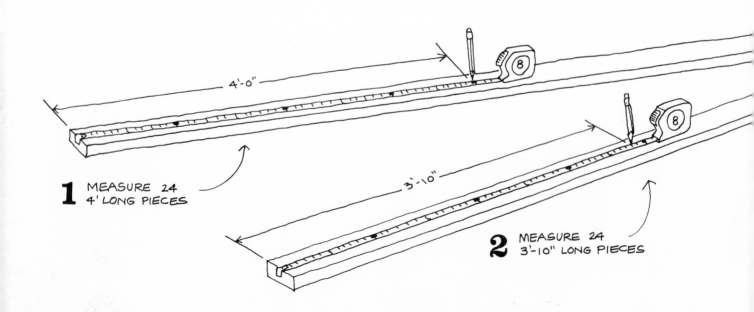

4'-0"

1 MEASURE 24 4' LONG PIECES

3'-10"

2 MEASURE 24 3'-10" LONG PIECES

Step 4
Sawing the Panel Frame Strips

After you've drawn a neat, straight line with your square at each measured pencil mark, you're ready to saw the panel frame strips. Saw them carefully because you'll be nailing the edges together later and it's important they be straight. After they're cut, stack the 3'-10" pieces separate from the 4' pieces, so they don't get mixed up (later) when you're building the frames.

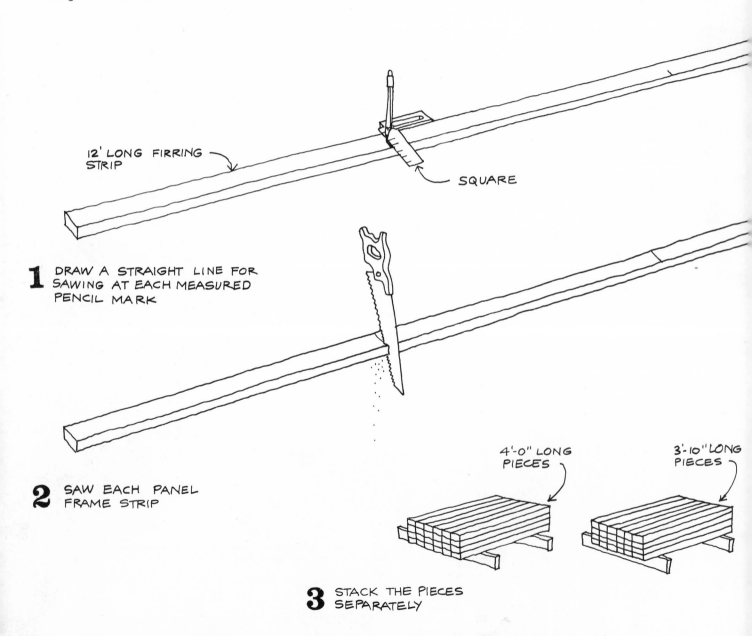

12' LONG FIRRING STRIP

SQUARE

1 DRAW A STRAIGHT LINE FOR SAWING AT EACH MEASURED PENCIL MARK

2 SAW EACH PANEL FRAME STRIP

4'-0" LONG PIECES

3'-10" LONG PIECES

3 STACK THE PIECES SEPARATELY

Step 5
Drilling the Panel Frame Strips

Next, drill four 1″ holes into each 3′-10″ long panel frame strip. These holes will be used later to hold the pegs when you attach the panels together to make your house. Since you must accurately drill into 24 of them, it's extremely important to drill one perfect panel frame strip and use it to lay out the other 23.

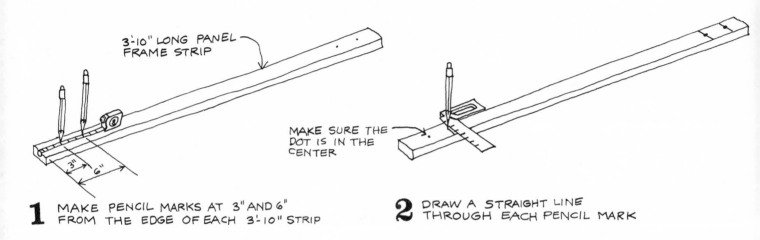

3′-10″ LONG PANEL
FRAME STRIP

MAKE SURE THE
DOT IS IN THE
CENTER

3″ 6″

1 MAKE PENCIL MARKS AT 3″ AND 6″
FROM THE EDGE OF EACH 3′-10″ STRIP

2 DRAW A STRAIGHT LINE
THROUGH EACH PENCIL MARK

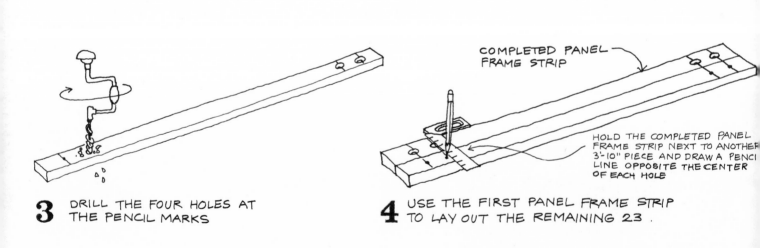

COMPLETED PANEL
FRAME STRIP

HOLD THE COMPLETED PANEL
FRAME STRIP NEXT TO ANOTHER
3′-10″ PIECE AND DRAW A PENCIL
LINE OPPOSITE THE CENTER
OF EACH HOLE

3 DRILL THE FOUR HOLES AT
THE PENCIL MARKS

4 USE THE FIRST PANEL FRAME STRIP
TO LAY OUT THE REMAINING 23 .

Step 6
Laying Out the Doors and Windows

You can lay out almost any shape for a window or a door on your panel sheets, but the circle and the square are the easiest to saw. So, here are the ways to lay out the circle and the square.

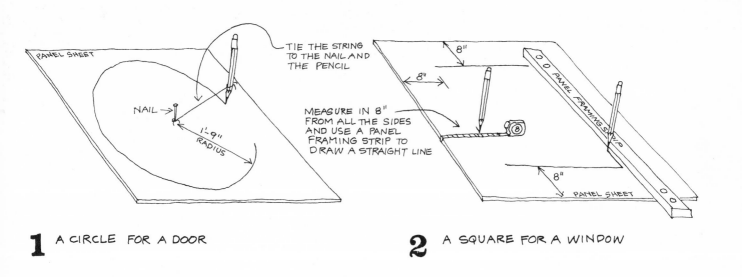

1 A CIRCLE FOR A DOOR

PANEL SHEET

NAIL →

1'-9" RADIUS

TIE THE STRING TO THE NAIL AND THE PENCIL

2 A SQUARE FOR A WINDOW

8"

8"

MEASURE IN 8" FROM ALL THE SIDES AND USE A PANEL FRAMING STRIP TO DRAW A STRAIGHT LINE

PANEL FRAMING STRIP

8"

PANEL SHEET

Here are some suggestions for doors and windows that you may want to draw on your panels.

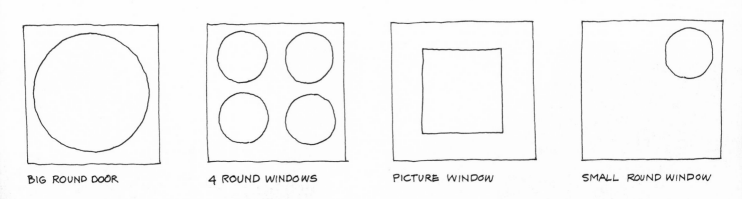

BIG ROUND DOOR   4 ROUND WINDOWS   PICTURE WINDOW   SMALL ROUND WINDOW

Step 7
Nailing the Panel Sheets to the Panel Frame

You're ready now to put the twelve panels together. First lay out a frame (made from two 3'-10" long strips and two 4' long strips) on the ground. Then flop a panel sheet over it and nail through the top of the sheet into the frame after you've carefully lined up the edges. Finally, drive two nails into the edge of each corner to make the frame stronger.

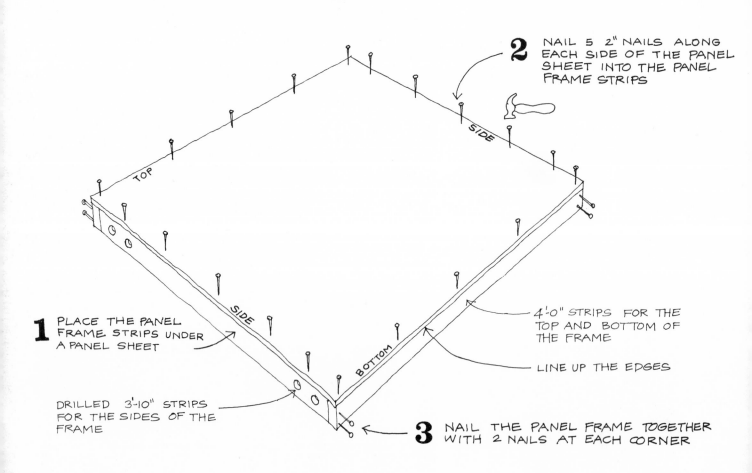

2 NAIL 5 2" NAILS ALONG EACH SIDE OF THE PANEL SHEET INTO THE PANEL FRAME STRIPS

TOP

SIDE

1 PLACE THE PANEL FRAME STRIPS UNDER A PANEL SHEET

SIDE

BOTTOM

4'-0" STRIPS FOR THE TOP AND BOTTOM OF THE FRAME

LINE UP THE EDGES

DRILLED 3'-10" STRIPS FOR THE SIDES OF THE FRAME

3 NAIL THE PANEL FRAME TOGETHER WITH 2 NAILS AT EACH CORNER

Step 8
Sawing Out the Windows and Doors

After you've put the panels together, you're ready to saw out the windows and doors. First, drill a hole inside the window or door area to start the keyhole saw. After the hole is drilled, stick the point of the keyhole saw into it and carefully saw around the pencil line.

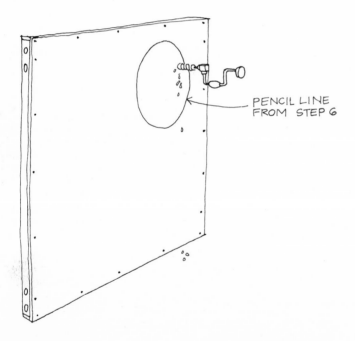

1 DRILL A HOLE INSIDE THE PENCIL LINE OF THE WINDOW OR DOOR

PENCIL LINE FROM STEP 6

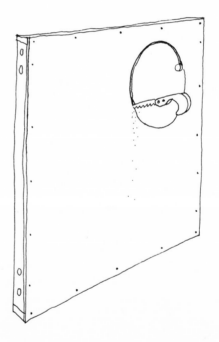

2 KEYHOLE SAW AROUND THE PENCIL LINE

Step 9
Painting the Panels

This job is easy and fun! Place a panel on four orange crates, get the paint roller wet, and roll an even coat of paint over the panel surface. Do this with each panel, laying each one on the ground to dry for at least three hours. Then roll on a second coat if necessary and allow the panels to dry again. Be sure to wear old clothes or a good apron since rollers sometimes spray paint.

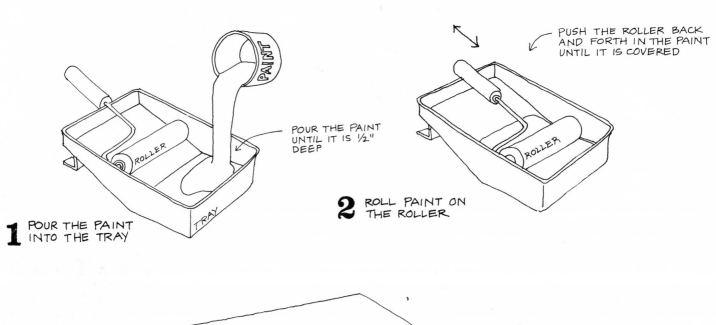

POUR THE PAINT UNTIL IT IS ½" DEEP

PUSH THE ROLLER BACK AND FORTH IN THE PAINT UNTIL IT IS COVERED

1 POUR THE PAINT INTO THE TRAY

2 ROLL PAINT ON THE ROLLER

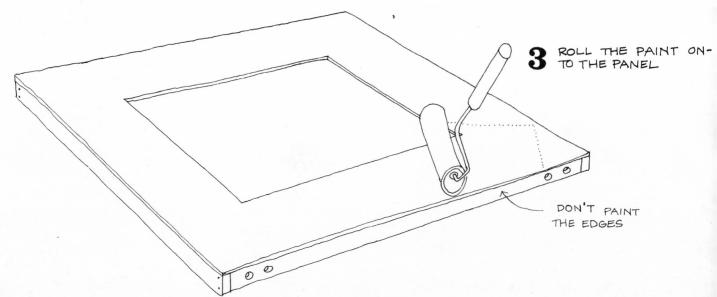

3 ROLL THE PAINT ONTO THE PANEL

DON'T PAINT THE EDGES

Step 10
Sawing and Drilling the Corner Posts

The corner post is the piece of wood that fits at the corner of each panel and holds one panel to another, with pegs. It's *very* important that the holes in the panel frame strip match up with the holes in the corner post or the pegs won't fit. It's best to make another panel frame strip and use it as a guide when you lay out the corner post holes.

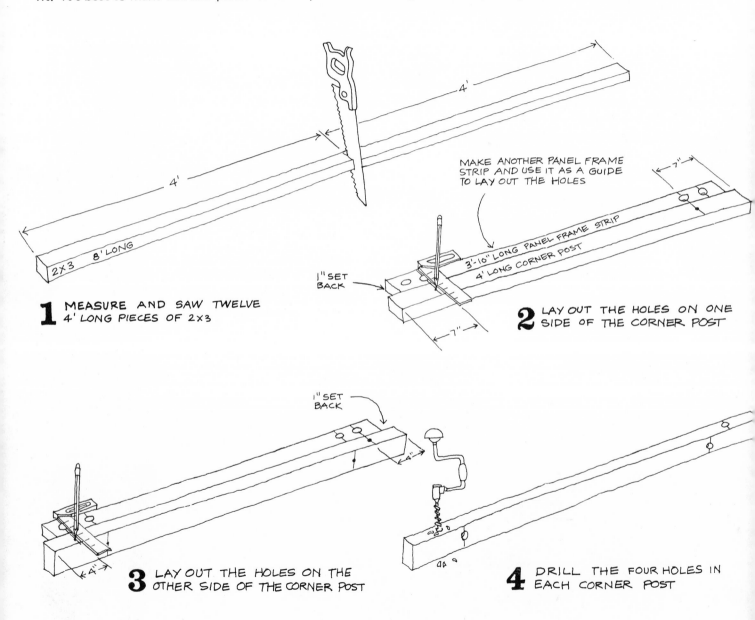

1 MEASURE AND SAW TWELVE 4' LONG PIECES OF 2x3

2 LAY OUT THE HOLES ON ONE SIDE OF THE CORNER POST

3 LAY OUT THE HOLES ON THE OTHER SIDE OF THE CORNER POST

4 DRILL THE FOUR HOLES IN EACH CORNER POST

Step 11
Sawing the Pegs

Next, saw twenty-seven 4″ long pegs from the three 1″ dowels. These pegs will fit tightly in the holes. Then saw twenty-seven 4″ long pegs from the 7/8″ dowels. These pegs will fit loosely in the holes.

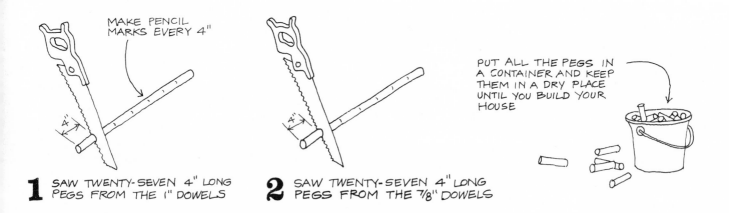

MAKE PENCIL MARKS EVERY 4″

PUT ALL THE PEGS IN A CONTAINER AND KEEP THEM IN A DRY PLACE UNTIL YOU BUILD YOUR HOUSE

1 SAW TWENTY-SEVEN 4″ LONG PEGS FROM THE 1″ DOWELS

2 SAW TWENTY-SEVEN 4″ LONG PEGS FROM THE 7/8″ DOWELS

Deliver the Parts to Your Site

If you haven't built the house parts near your site, get a friend to help carry and stack them at a place a few feet from where you plan to build.

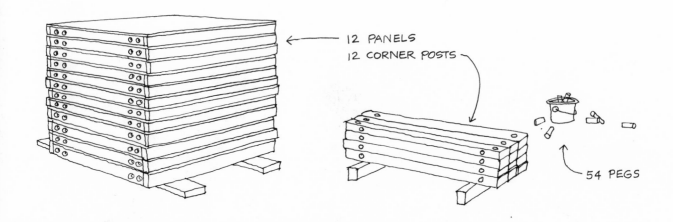

12 PANELS
12 CORNER POSTS

54 PEGS

Step 12
Designing a Shape for Your House

Now you must figure out a shape for your house. Just lean one panel against another to make a corner and continue leaning panels and making corners until you've enclosed the house. Moving these light panels around is so easy that you should try many *different* designs until you've decided on the best. Make sure to put the door panel facing the entry and the window panels facing the views you want.

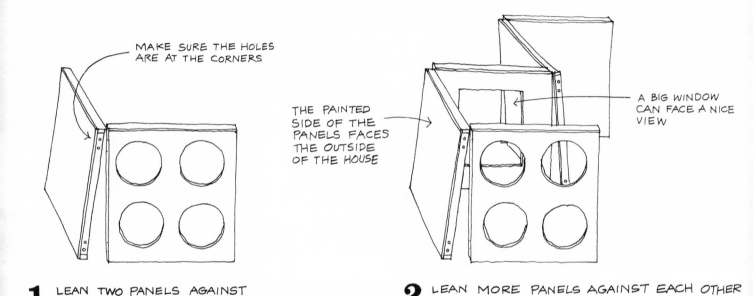

MAKE SURE THE HOLES ARE AT THE CORNERS

THE PAINTED SIDE OF THE PANELS FACES THE OUTSIDE OF THE HOUSE

A BIG WINDOW CAN FACE A NICE VIEW

1 LEAN TWO PANELS AGAINST EACH OTHER TO MAKE A CORNER

2 LEAN MORE PANELS AGAINST EACH OTHER UNTIL YOU HAVE A SHAPE THAT YOU LIKE

Here are some ideas for shapes to try on your site. Maybe you can design a better one.

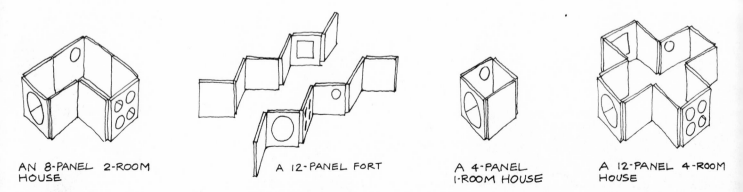

AN 8-PANEL 2-ROOM HOUSE

A 12-PANEL FORT

A 4-PANEL 1-ROOM HOUSE

A 12-PANEL 4-ROOM HOUSE

Step 13
Building Your House

Once you've arranged your panels into a shape you like, all that remains to be done is to connect the corners. This is done by hammering pegs through a corner post and into the holes in the panels.

After you've pegged the corners, invite your friends over to see your factory-built house.

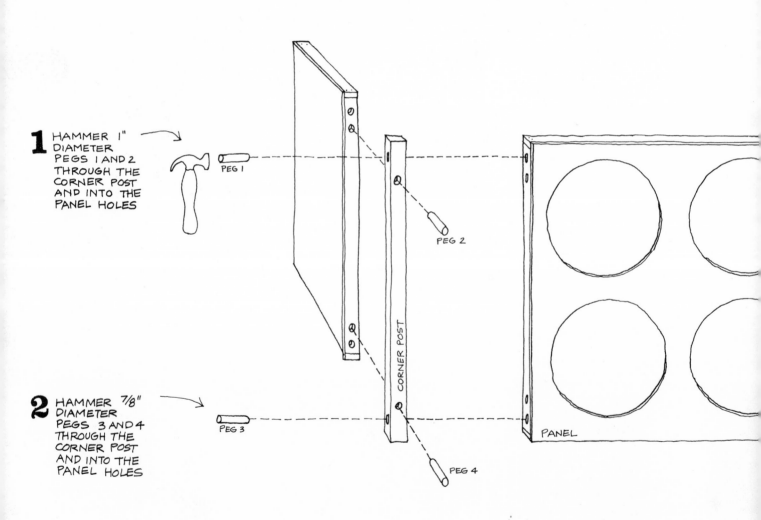

1 HAMMER 1" DIAMETER PEGS 1 AND 2 THROUGH THE CORNER POST AND INTO THE PANEL HOLES

PEG 1

PEG 2

CORNER POST

2 HAMMER 7/8" DIAMETER PEGS 3 AND 4 THROUGH THE CORNER POST AND INTO THE PANEL HOLES

PEG 3

PEG 4

PANEL

The Glass House

After 1930, Americans began to put more and more glass into the walls of their houses. Picture windows, bay windows, and skylights became popular. Many people who owned relatively large pieces of land even built all-glass houses using the trees around them for privacy.

Our house is modeled after these all-glass houses except that we've made a see-through glass roof. As you can see in the photograph on the next page, we've used clear plastic instead of glass. But if you stretch it real tight, it seems just like glass, and it doesn't shatter.

After you're finished building the glass house, you may want to hang clear plastic drapes over the doorways to trap the heat from the sun's rays. If you locate your house in the sun, it will be warm even in the winter. Heat from the sun is known as solar energy.

A good book on solar energy for houses is the *Energy Primer* by the Portola Institute (see the Appendix).

You'll also be able to use your glass house as an excellent greenhouse for plants in the early spring. If you add a stone floor inside, the stones will absorb the heat from the sun during the day and give off heat during the night, keeping the plants warm.

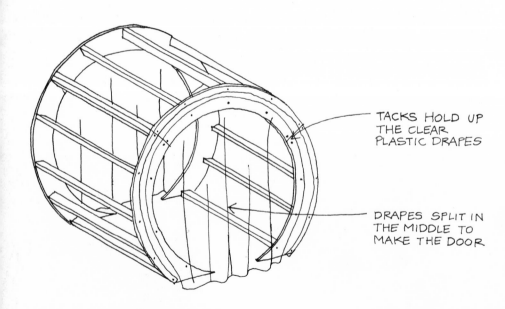

TACKS HOLD UP
THE CLEAR
PLASTIC DRAPES

DRAPES SPLIT IN
THE MIDDLE TO
MAKE THE DOOR

Step 1
Assembling the Tools

Here's a list of tools you'll need to build the glass house. Assemble them on your workbench and check to make sure they're working well before you start.

1 HAMMER
FOR NAILING

3 KEYHOLE SAW
FOR CUTTING THE CURVES
IN THE PLYWOOD

5 TAPE
FOR MEASURING A
MATERIAL TO THE
RIGHT SIZE

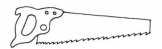

2 CROSS-CUT SAW
FOR CUTTING THE WOOD
STRIPS TO THE RIGHT
LENGTH

4 SQUARE
FOR MAKING A
STRAIGHT LINE
ON THE WOOD STRIPS
BEFORE SAWING

6 BANDAGES
FOR CUTS

7 APRON
FOR HOLDING
NAILS

Step 2
Assembling the Materials

Here's a list of materials you'll need to build the glass house. Your local lumber yard has these materials and should be happy to deliver them to you.

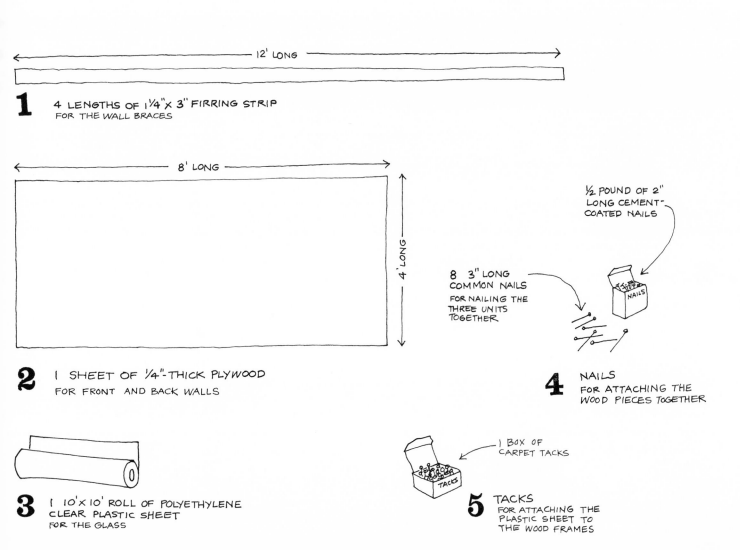

1 4 LENGTHS OF 1¼" X 3" FIRRING STRIP
FOR THE WALL BRACES

12' LONG

2 1 SHEET OF ¼"-THICK PLYWOOD
FOR FRONT AND BACK WALLS

8' LONG

4' LONG

3 1 10'X 10' ROLL OF POLYETHYLENE
CLEAR PLASTIC SHEET
FOR THE GLASS

½ POUND OF 2" LONG CEMENT-COATED NAILS

8 3" LONG COMMON NAILS
FOR NAILING THE THREE UNITS TOGETHER

4 NAILS
FOR ATTACHING THE WOOD PIECES TOGETHER

1 BOX OF CARPET TACKS

5 TACKS
FOR ATTACHING THE PLASTIC SHEET TO THE WOOD FRAMES

Step 3
Laying Out and Sawing the Frame Pieces

The third step in building the glass house is to make the 6 curved frame pieces from the ¼" thick sheet of plywood. Carefully follow the directions below and lay out the first frame piece at the top of the plywood sheet. Then, saw it out, and use it as a pattern for the remaining 5 framing pieces.

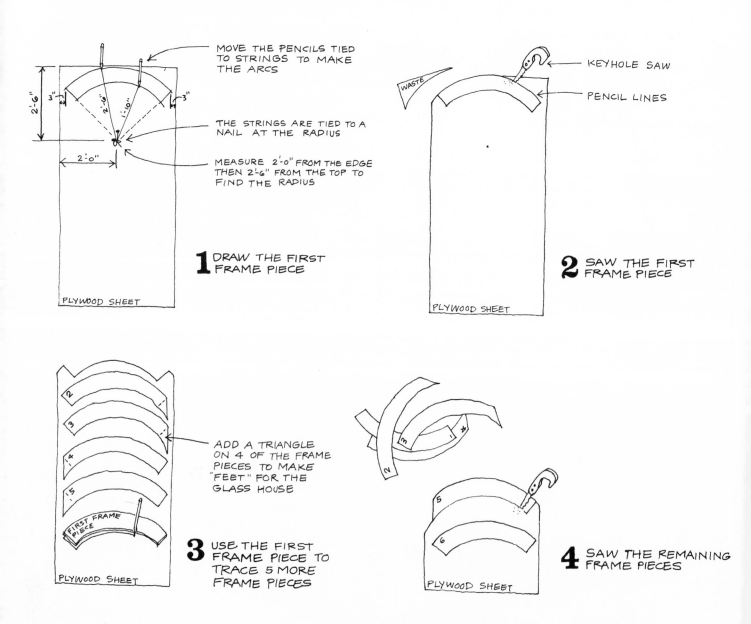

MOVE THE PENCILS TIED TO STRINGS TO MAKE THE ARCS

THE STRINGS ARE TIED TO A NAIL AT THE RADIUS

MEASURE 2'-0" FROM THE EDGE THEN 2'-6" FROM THE TOP TO FIND THE RADIUS

1 DRAW THE FIRST FRAME PIECE

PLYWOOD SHEET

KEYHOLE SAW

PENCIL LINES

WASTE

2 SAW THE FIRST FRAME PIECE

PLYWOOD SHEET

ADD A TRIANGLE ON 4 OF THE FRAME PIECES TO MAKE "FEET" FOR THE GLASS HOUSE

FIRST FRAME PIECE

3 USE THE FIRST FRAME PIECE TO TRACE 5 MORE FRAME PIECES

PLYWOOD SHEET

4 SAW THE REMAINING FRAME PIECES

PLYWOOD SHEET

110

Step 4
Building the Three Frames

The 3 frames for the glass house are built using the plywood framing pieces you've just made plus 12 braces cut from the firring strips. Just carefully follow the directions below.

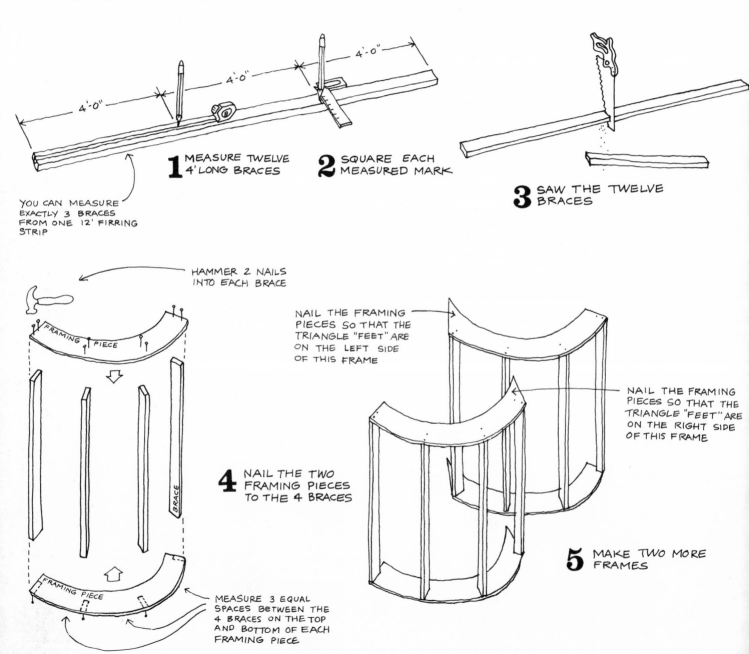

1 MEASURE TWELVE 4' LONG BRACES

YOU CAN MEASURE EXACTLY 3 BRACES FROM ONE 12' FIRRING STRIP

4'-0" 4'-0" 4'-0"

2 SQUARE EACH MEASURED MARK

3 SAW THE TWELVE BRACES

HAMMER 2 NAILS INTO EACH BRACE

FRAMING PIECE

BRACE

FRAMING PIECE

4 NAIL THE TWO FRAMING PIECES TO THE 4 BRACES

MEASURE 3 EQUAL SPACES BETWEEN THE 4 BRACES ON THE TOP AND BOTTOM OF EACH FRAMING PIECE

NAIL THE FRAMING PIECES SO THAT THE TRIANGLE "FEET" ARE ON THE LEFT SIDE OF THIS FRAME

NAIL THE FRAMING PIECES SO THAT THE TRIANGLE "FEET" ARE ON THE RIGHT SIDE OF THIS FRAME

5 MAKE TWO MORE FRAMES

Step 5
Stretching the Clear Plastic Over the Frames

The "glass" in the glass house is made from clear plastic sheets that are stretched over the 3 frames you've just built. You'll need a friend to stretch the plastic as you tack it in place. Remember not to stretch it too hard or it will tear. Just get it tight. Believe it or not, after your glass house is built, the rain will shrink the plastic even tighter, so it will look like glass.

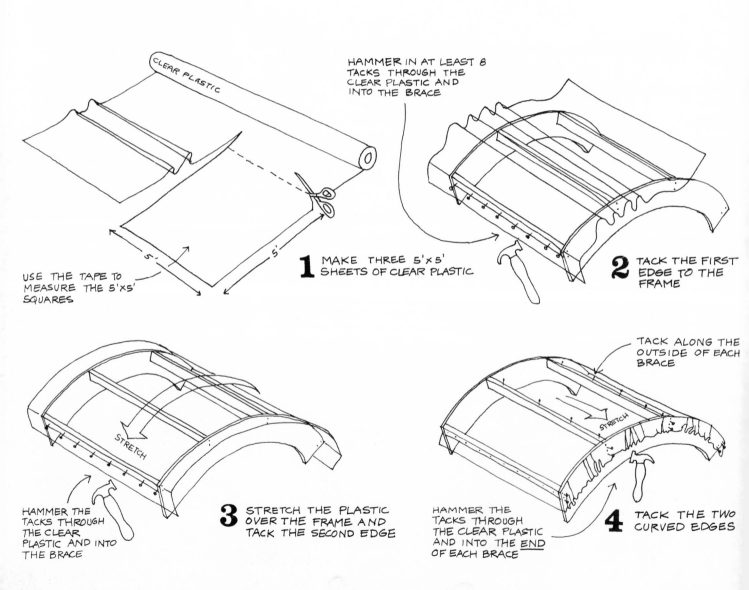

HAMMER IN AT LEAST 8 TACKS THROUGH THE CLEAR PLASTIC AND INTO THE BRACE

CLEAR PLASTIC

USE THE TAPE TO MEASURE THE 5'x5' SQUARES

1 MAKE THREE 5'x5' SHEETS OF CLEAR PLASTIC

2 TACK THE FIRST EDGE TO THE FRAME

HAMMER THE TACKS THROUGH THE CLEAR PLASTIC AND INTO THE BRACE

3 STRETCH THE PLASTIC OVER THE FRAME AND TACK THE SECOND EDGE

TACK ALONG THE OUTSIDE OF EACH BRACE

HAMMER THE TACKS THROUGH THE CLEAR PLASTIC AND INTO THE END OF EACH BRACE

4 TACK THE TWO CURVED EDGES

Step 6
Attaching the Frames

Have a few friends help you lift the top frame and hold it steady over the 2 side frames as you stand inside the house and hammer them together with nails through the end braces. This house is rather delicate so don't attempt to move it very much after you've put the frames together.

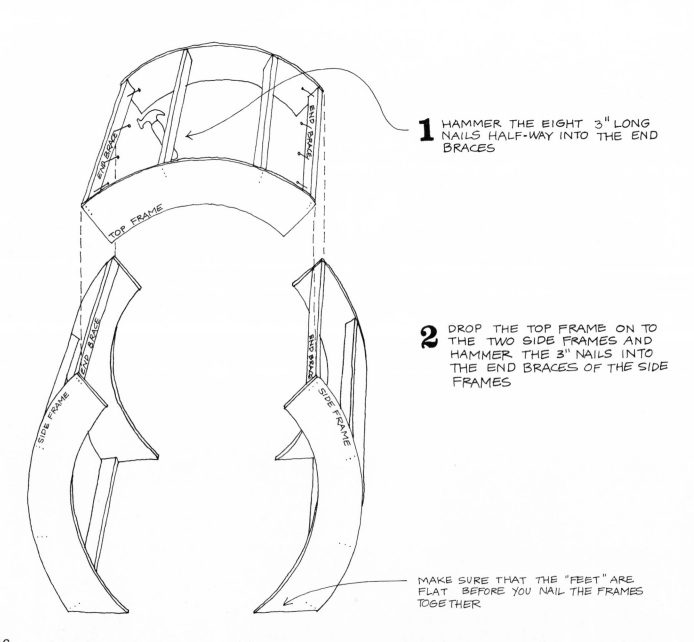

1 HAMMER THE EIGHT 3" LONG NAILS HALF-WAY INTO THE END BRACES

2 DROP THE TOP FRAME ON TO THE TWO SIDE FRAMES AND HAMMER THE 3" NAILS INTO THE END BRACES OF THE SIDE FRAMES

MAKE SURE THAT THE "FEET" ARE FLAT BEFORE YOU NAIL THE FRAMES TOGETHER

The Post & Beam House

The earliest houses built by American settlers were made from posts and beams cut from logs. The logs were stripped of their branches, and the round sides squared with an axe. Then the joints were cut and peg holes were drilled into the end of each post and beam.

Once all of these posts and beams were made, the builder would invite all his friends to a house-raising party. Everyone would work all day until the frame of the house was pegged together and ready for the builder to attach the siding, roofing, doors, and windows. A good book on this subject is *Build Your Own Early American Village* by Forrest Wilson (see the Appendix).

Our post and beam house is exactly the same as the early Americans' except that we're lucky enough today to be able to buy the posts and beams already squared and cut to the proper length by the lumber yard.

This house requires the most work. It's very hard sawing all of the lap joints and drilling the holes. But when you finish the joints, you can invite all your friends to your own house-raising party. They'll be amazed when they see your house fit together like a giant wooden puzzle.

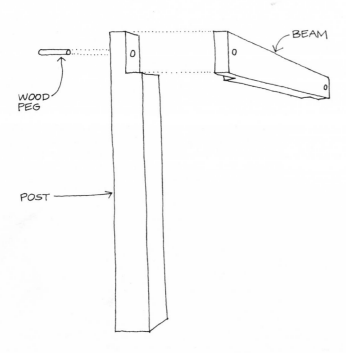

WOOD PEG

BEAM

POST

Step 1
Assembling the Tools

Here's a list of the tools you'll need to build the post and beam house. Make sure the crosscut saw and the drill bit are sharp since you'll be doing a lot of heavy work with both tools.

1 HAMMER
FOR NAILING AND
DRIVING IN THE PEGS

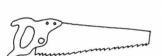

2 CROSSCUT SAW
FOR CUTTING THE WOOD

3 LEVEL
FOR LEVELING THE BASE SO
THAT THE HOUSE IS STRAIGHT

4 KEYHOLE SAW
FOR CUTTING OUT WINDOWS
IN THE SIDING

5 BRACE AND BIT
FOR DRILLING PEG
HOLES

6 SQUARE
FOR MARKING A
STRAIGHT LINE
ON WOOD THAT
IS TO BE SAWED

7 TAPE
FOR MEASURING A
MATERIAL TO THE
RIGHT SIZE

8 BANDAGES
FOR CUTS

9 CARPENTER'S
APRON
FOR HOLDING
NAILS

Step 2
Assembling the Materials

This list of materials is a bit too complicated to phone your lumber yard for delivery. Give the yard a copy of this page and let the people there have a day or two to saw and deliver the pieces. You may want to use rough-cut wood for the 4"x4" pieces and the 2"x4" roof rafters, as we did, but remember it's much more work. Rough-cut wood is usually wet inside and it's always wider (it hasn't been planed smooth yet) making for more difficult sawing and drilling.

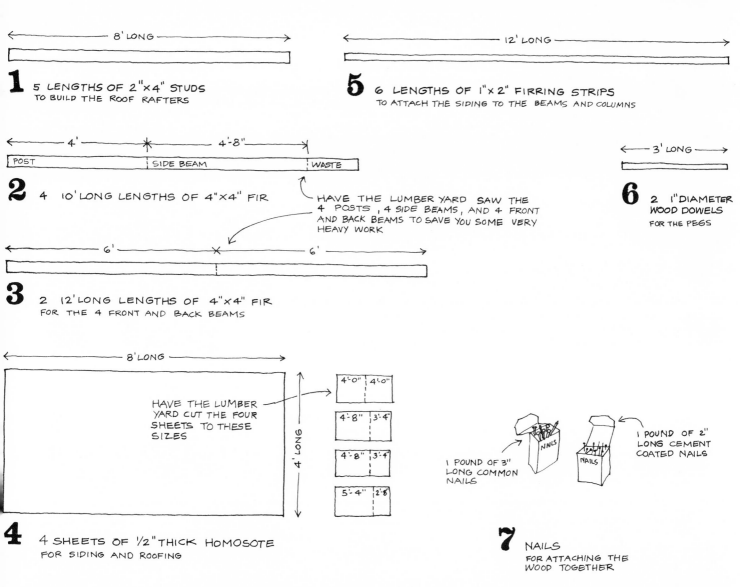

1 5 LENGTHS OF 2"x4" STUDS
TO BUILD THE ROOF RAFTERS

2 4 10'LONG LENGTHS OF 4"x4" FIR

HAVE THE LUMBER YARD SAW THE
4 POSTS, 4 SIDE BEAMS, AND 4 FRONT
AND BACK BEAMS TO SAVE YOU SOME VERY
HEAVY WORK

3 2 12'LONG LENGTHS OF 4"x4" FIR
FOR THE 4 FRONT AND BACK BEAMS

4 4 SHEETS OF 1/2"THICK HOMOSOTE
FOR SIDING AND ROOFING

HAVE THE LUMBER
YARD CUT THE FOUR
SHEETS TO THESE
SIZES

5 6 LENGTHS OF 1"x 2" FIRRING STRIPS
TO ATTACH THE SIDING TO THE BEAMS AND COLUMNS

6 2 1"DIAMETER
WOOD DOWELS
FOR THE PEGS

7 NAILS
FOR ATTACHING THE
WOOD TOGETHER

1 POUND OF 3"
LONG COMMON
NAILS

1 POUND OF 2"
LONG CEMENT
COATED NAILS

Step 3
Sawing the Lap Joints

The lap joints are the notches you saw in the ends of each beam. The sawing of these joints will be very hard work. Don't expect to finish in one day. If your hand starts to get sore, wear a glove and, if you get really tired, ask your friends to help. Everybody likes to saw.

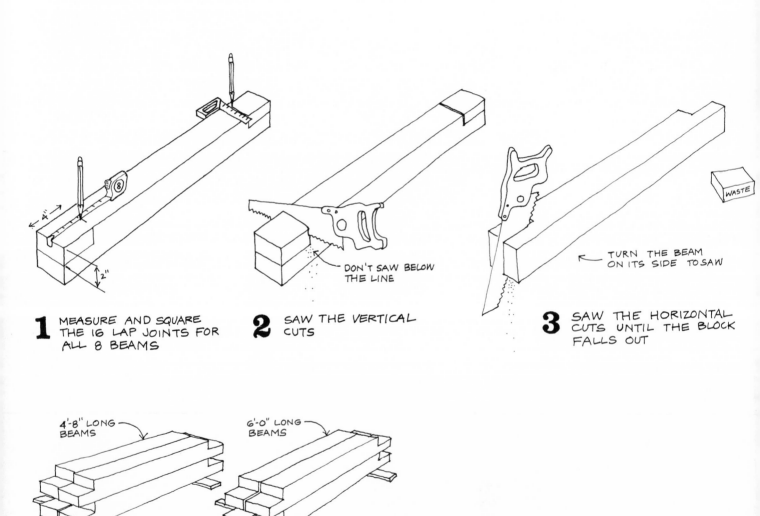

1 MEASURE AND SQUARE THE 16 LAP JOINTS FOR ALL 8 BEAMS

4"

2"

2 SAW THE VERTICAL CUTS

DON'T SAW BELOW THE LINE

3 SAW THE HORIZONTAL CUTS UNTIL THE BLOCK FALLS OUT

TURN THE BEAM ON ITS SIDE TO SAW

WASTE

4'-8" LONG BEAMS

6'-0" LONG BEAMS

4 STACK THE BEAMS SEPARATELY

Step 4
Attaching the Nailer Strips

The nailer strips are the pieces of wood that provide a ledge to nail the siding to the house. If you turn to page 138 you can see the siding being nailed to these strips.

You'll need four 4' long nailer strips, four 5'-4'' long nailer strips, and eight 3'-10'' long nailer strips. Carefully measure and saw them from the 6 lengths of 1''x2'' firring strip before nailing them to the posts and beams.

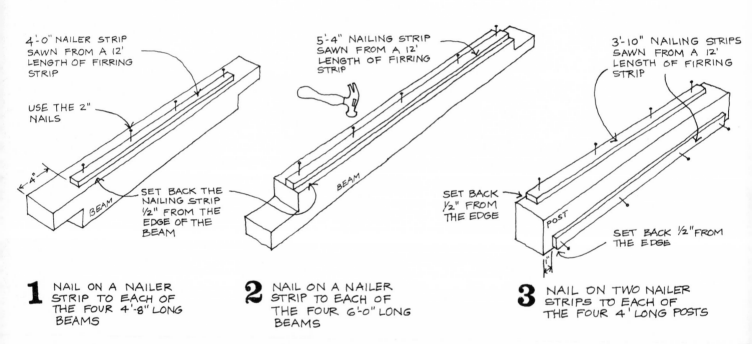

4'-0" NAILER STRIP SAWN FROM A 12' LENGTH OF FIRRING STRIP

USE THE 2" NAILS

SET BACK THE NAILING STRIP ½" FROM THE EDGE OF THE BEAM

5'-4" NAILING STRIP SAWN FROM A 12' LENGTH OF FIRRING STRIP

3'-10" NAILING STRIPS SAWN FROM A 12' LENGTH OF FIRRING STRIP

SET BACK ½" FROM THE EDGE

SET BACK ½" FROM THE EDGE

1 NAIL ON A NAILER STRIP TO EACH OF THE FOUR 4'-8" LONG BEAMS

2 NAIL ON A NAILER STRIP TO EACH OF THE FOUR 6'-0" LONG BEAMS

3 NAIL ON TWO NAILER STRIPS TO EACH OF THE FOUR 4' LONG POSTS

Step 5
Drilling the Peg Holes and Sawing the Pegs

A 7″-long peg will be hammered into the hole in each lap joint to hold the frame together when you erect the house. If you turn to page 132 you'll see how the pegs work. It's important to drill the holes as straight as you can.

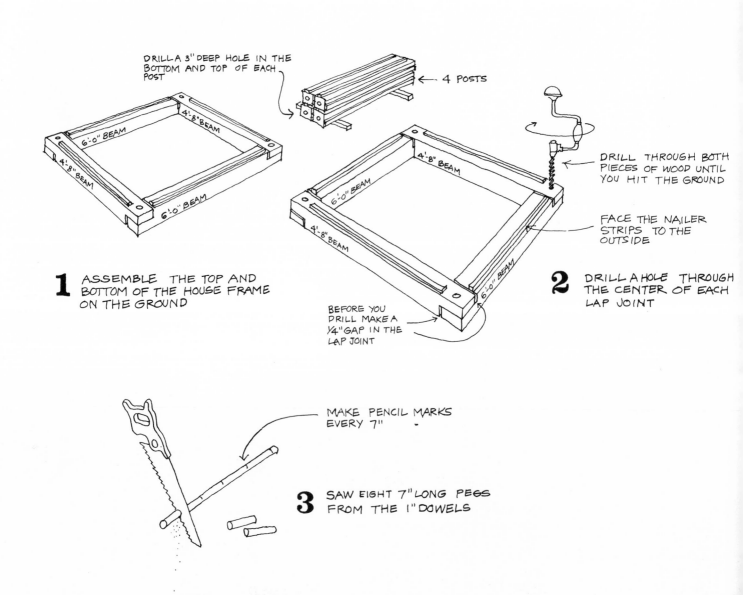

DRILL A 3″ DEEP HOLE IN THE BOTTOM AND TOP OF EACH POST

← 4 POSTS

6'-0" BEAM
4'-8" BEAM
4'-8" BEAM
6'-0" BEAM

4'-8" BEAM
6'-0" BEAM
4'-8" BEAM
6'-0" BEAM

DRILL THROUGH BOTH PIECES OF WOOD UNTIL YOU HIT THE GROUND

FACE THE NAILER STRIPS TO THE OUTSIDE

1 ASSEMBLE THE TOP AND BOTTOM OF THE HOUSE FRAME ON THE GROUND

BEFORE YOU DRILL MAKE A ¼″ GAP IN THE LAP JOINT

2 DRILL A HOLE THROUGH THE CENTER OF EACH LAP JOINT

MAKE PENCIL MARKS EVERY 7″

3 SAW EIGHT 7″ LONG PEGS FROM THE 1″ DOWELS

Step 6
Laying Out and Sawing the Windows

Now you're ready to lay out and saw the windows in the Homosote panels. Just follow the instructions below and carefully pencil the window locations on the panels. Saw along the pencil lines.

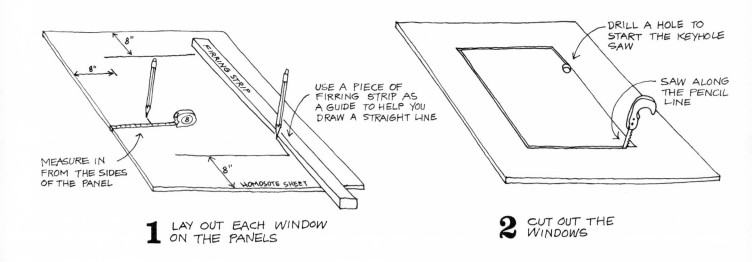

1 LAY OUT EACH WINDOW ON THE PANELS

MEASURE IN FROM THE SIDES OF THE PANEL

USE A PIECE OF FIRRING STRIP AS A GUIDE TO HELP YOU DRAW A STRAIGHT LINE

FIRRING STRIP

HOMOSOTE SHEET

2 CUT OUT THE WINDOWS

DRILL A HOLE TO START THE KEYHOLE SAW

SAW ALONG THE PENCIL LINE

Here are the dimensions for the window layout used in the house shown in the photographs. Remember: these panels have already been cut to size at your lumber yard. All you need to do is cut in the windows.

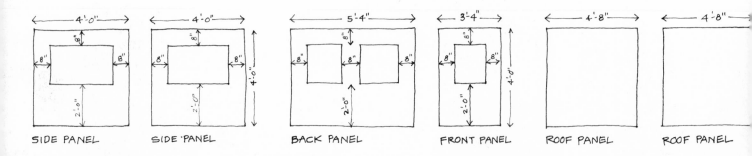

SIDE PANEL   SIDE PANEL   BACK PANEL   FRONT PANEL   ROOF PANEL   ROOF PANEL

Step 7
Sawing the Roof Rafters

The easiest way to make the roof rafters is to saw out one perfect rafter and use it as a pattern to trace the rest. Take your time while sawing the angles. It is important they be straight, clean saw cuts.

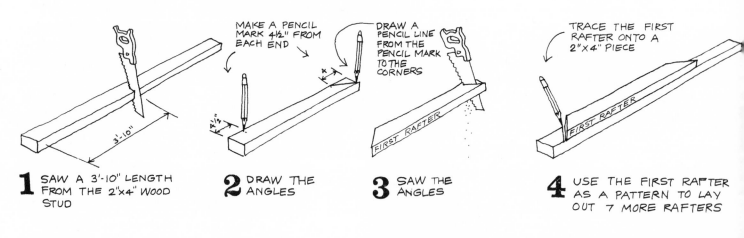

MAKE A PENCIL MARK 4½" FROM EACH END

DRAW A PENCIL LINE FROM THE PENCIL MARK TO THE CORNERS

TRACE THE FIRST RAFTER ONTO A 2"X4" PIECE

FIRST RAFTER

3'-10"

4½"

FIRST RAFTER

1 SAW A 3'-10" LENGTH FROM THE 2"X4" WOOD STUD

2 DRAW THE ANGLES

3 SAW THE ANGLES

4 USE THE FIRST RAFTER AS A PATTERN TO LAY OUT 7 MORE RAFTERS

REPEAT THESE STEPS UNTIL YOU HAVE MADE EIGHT RAFTERS

Step 8
Gathering the Parts at Your Site

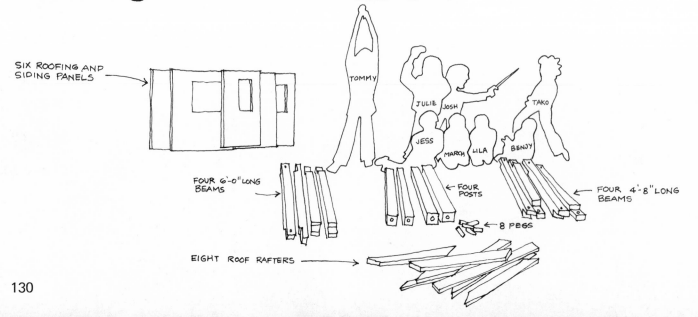

SIX ROOFING AND SIDING PANELS

TOMMY

JULIE

JOSH

JESS

MARCH

LILA

BENJY

TAKO

FOUR 6'-0" LONG BEAMS

FOUR POSTS

FOUR 4'-8" LONG BEAMS

8 PEGS

EIGHT ROOF RAFTERS

130

Step 9
Raising the Frame

You'll need a ladder and a friend or two to help you assemble the heavy posts and beams into the house frame. You can use the ladder to stand on to help you guide the top beams onto their pegs. And you'll need your friends to help lift the posts and beams into place.

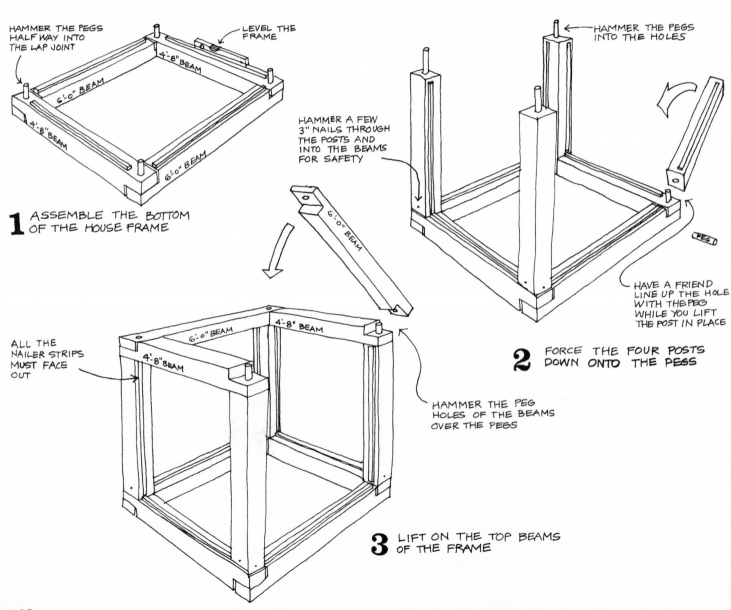

HAMMER THE PEGS HALFWAY INTO THE LAP JOINT

LEVEL THE FRAME

4'-8" BEAM

6'-0" BEAM

4'-8" BEAM

6'-0" BEAM

1 ASSEMBLE THE BOTTOM OF THE HOUSE FRAME

HAMMER THE PEGS INTO THE HOLES

HAMMER A FEW 3" NAILS THROUGH THE POSTS AND INTO THE BEAMS FOR SAFETY

6'-0" BEAM

PEG

HAVE A FRIEND LINE UP THE HOLE WITH THE PEG WHILE YOU LIFT THE POST IN PLACE

2 FORCE THE FOUR POSTS DOWN ONTO THE PEGS

ALL THE NAILER STRIPS MUST FACE OUT

6'-0" BEAM

4'-8" BEAM

4'-8" BEAM

HAMMER THE PEG HOLES OF THE BEAMS OVER THE PEGS

3 LIFT ON THE TOP BEAMS OF THE FRAME

Step 10
Attaching the Roof Rafters

You'll find it easiest to begin framing the roof by nailing the first 4 rafters to the king post on the ground. Have a friend help you lift this assembly onto the house frame. Nail it in place and attach the remaining rafters as shown below.

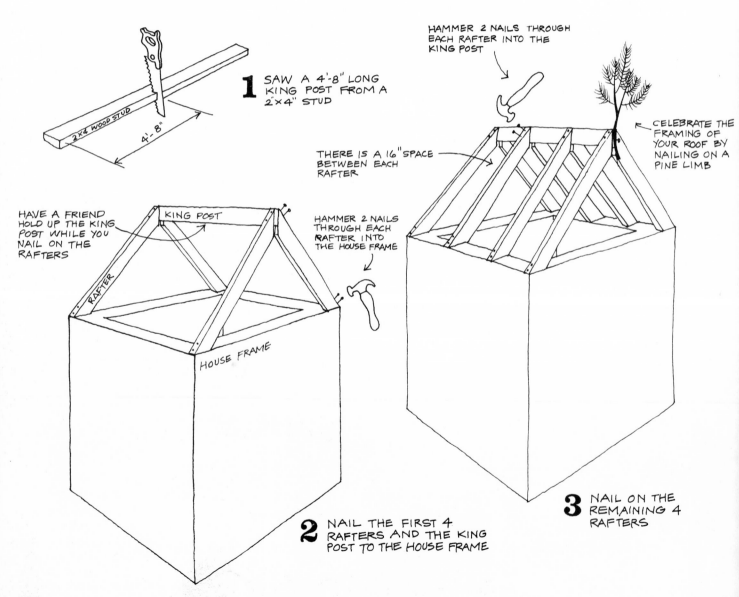

1 SAW A 4'-8" LONG KING POST FROM A 2"×4" STUD

2×4 WOOD STUD

4'-8"

HAVE A FRIEND HOLD UP THE KING POST WHILE YOU NAIL ON THE RAFTERS

KING POST

RAFTER

HOUSE FRAME

HAMMER 2 NAILS THROUGH EACH RAFTER INTO THE HOUSE FRAME

2 NAIL THE FIRST 4 RAFTERS AND THE KING POST TO THE HOUSE FRAME

HAMMER 2 NAILS THROUGH EACH RAFTER INTO THE KING POST

THERE IS A 16" SPACE BETWEEN EACH RAFTER

CELEBRATE THE FRAMING OF YOUR ROOF BY NAILING ON A PINE LIMB

3 NAIL ON THE REMAINING 4 RAFTERS

Step 11
Attaching the Roofing and Siding

The last step in building your post and beam house is attaching the roofing and siding to the frame. Before nailing, hold each panel into its place to make sure it fits. You may have to trim a panel with the saw if it's too tight. Once you're sure the panel is the perfect size, nail it to the nailer strips with the 2" nails all along the edge of the panel.

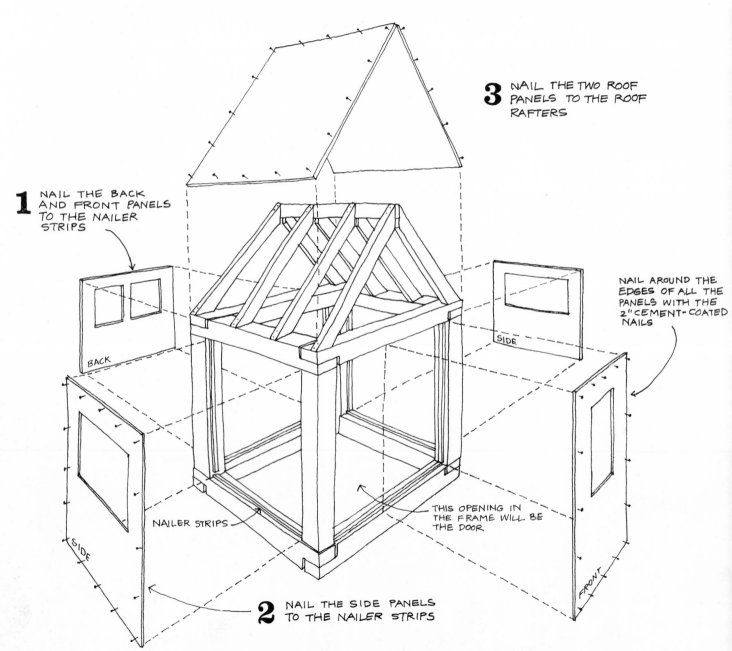

3 NAIL THE TWO ROOF PANELS TO THE ROOF RAFTERS

1 NAIL THE BACK AND FRONT PANELS TO THE NAILER STRIPS

NAIL AROUND THE EDGES OF ALL THE PANELS WITH THE 2" CEMENT-COATED NAILS

BACK

SIDE

NAILER STRIPS

THIS OPENING IN THE FRAME WILL BE THE DOOR

SIDE

FRONT

2 NAIL THE SIDE PANELS TO THE NAILER STRIPS

The Junkyard House

Recently we've learned that America is running short of natural resources and so we should learn to re-use or recycle waste materials. Many industries and universities are now working hard on this problem. And many young house-builders have found the junkyard an excellent place to gather free housebuilding materials. An excellent book about recycling building materials is *Shelter* by Shelter Publications (see the Appendix).

Our junkyard house is made from a collection of discarded parts found at the Woodstock, New York, town dump. The parts that you collect, whether from your junkyard or just off the street, will be different, naturally. And you'll have to use your imagination to figure out ways to connect the parts together. That's the fun of this house. At the start you don't know how it's going to grow. The idea is to collect and build, collect and build, collect and build, and collect and build.

This can be the most dangerous house for you to build. Make sure you don't cut yourself on sharp objects by wearing thick clothing and gloves. Be careful.

Step 1
Assembling the Tools

This house should be a cinch to build since all you do is attach junkyard materials together. You may be able to build your whole house with just a hammer and a few nails. If you need to saw any wooden materials that are too big, use the crosscut saw.

1 HAMMER
FOR NAILING

2 CROSSCUT SAW
FOR SAWING WOOD

3 BANDAGES
FOR CUTS

4 APRON
FOR HOLDING NAILS

Step 2
Collecting the Junk

Gather your junk from the junkyard or from the streets of your neighborhood. Stack it in piles at your site.

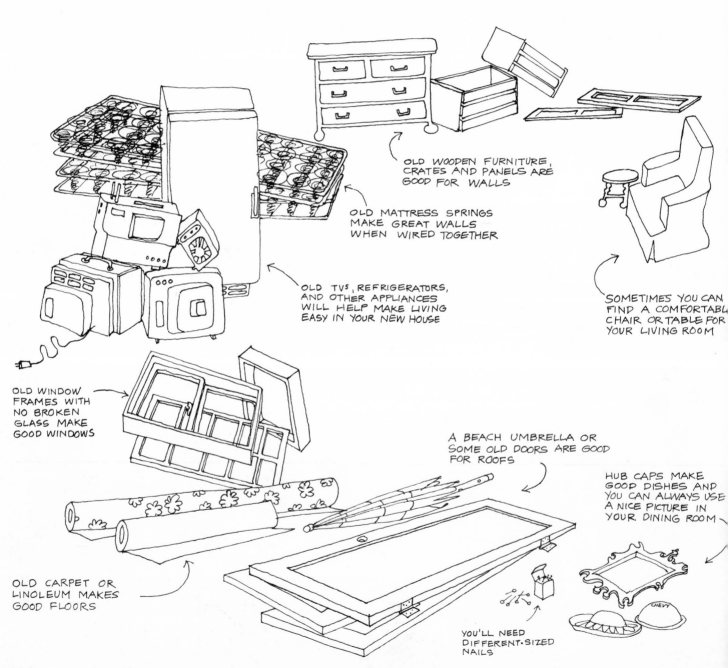

OLD WOODEN FURNITURE, CRATES AND PANELS ARE GOOD FOR WALLS

OLD MATTRESS SPRINGS MAKE GREAT WALLS WHEN WIRED TOGETHER

OLD TVs, REFRIGERATORS, AND OTHER APPLIANCES WILL HELP MAKE LIVING EASY IN YOUR NEW HOUSE

SOMETIMES YOU CAN FIND A COMFORTABL CHAIR OR TABLE FOR YOUR LIVING ROOM

OLD WINDOW FRAMES WITH NO BROKEN GLASS MAKE GOOD WINDOWS

A BEACH UMBRELLA OR SOME OLD DOORS ARE GOOD FOR ROOFS

HUB CAPS MAKE GOOD DISHES AND YOU CAN ALWAYS USE A NICE PICTURE IN YOUR DINING ROOM

OLD CARPET OR LINOLEUM MAKES GOOD FLOORS

YOU'LL NEED DIFFERENT-SIZED NAILS

Step 3
Building the First Room

The first room of your junkyard house must be as strong as you can make it because you'll be attaching and leaning other rooms to it as you build. Wire mattress frames make very strong, high walls for a first room. If you can't find some of these, use plywood or other lumber and give the first room strength by attaching it to a tree or the wall of a building.

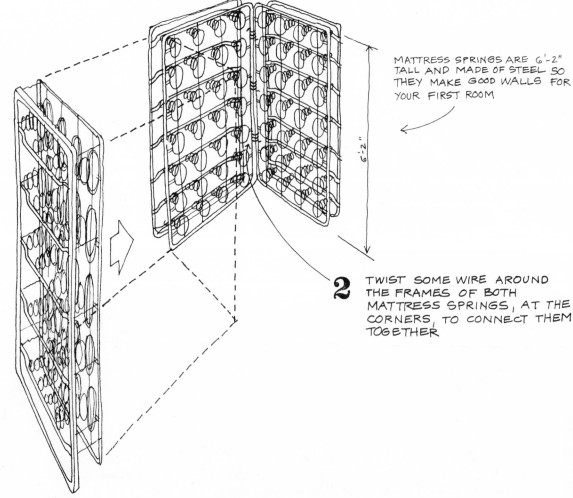

1 LEAN THE MATTRESS SPRINGS AGAINST EACH OTHER

MATTRESS SPRINGS ARE 6'-2" TALL AND MADE OF STEEL SO THEY MAKE GOOD WALLS FOR YOUR FIRST ROOM

6'-2"

2 TWIST SOME WIRE AROUND THE FRAMES OF BOTH MATTRESS SPRINGS, AT THE CORNERS, TO CONNECT THEM TOGETHER

Step 4
Adding More Rooms

Start adding more rooms by making walls around areas next to your first room.

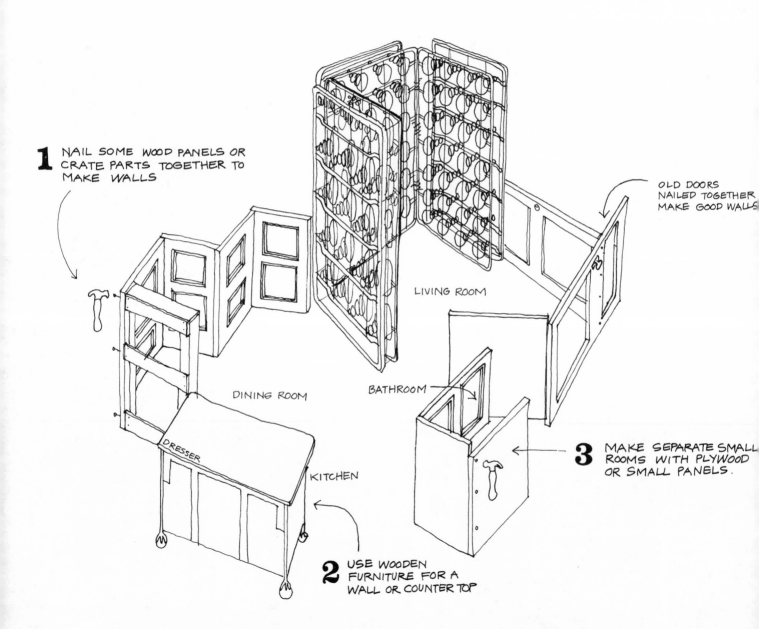

1 NAIL SOME WOOD PANELS OR CRATE PARTS TOGETHER TO MAKE WALLS

OLD DOORS NAILED TOGETHER MAKE GOOD WALLS

LIVING ROOM

DINING ROOM

BATHROOM

DRESSER

KITCHEN

3 MAKE SEPARATE SMALL ROOMS WITH PLYWOOD OR SMALL PANELS.

2 USE WOODEN FURNITURE FOR A WALL OR COUNTER TOP

Step 5
Building the Windows and Doors

Stand inside the walls of your house to find the best views. Then attach your old windows to see these views. Try to make a good strong front door since you'll be using it a lot. If you're lucky you'll be able to find an old hinged kitchen cabinet door ready to be nailed to one of your walls.

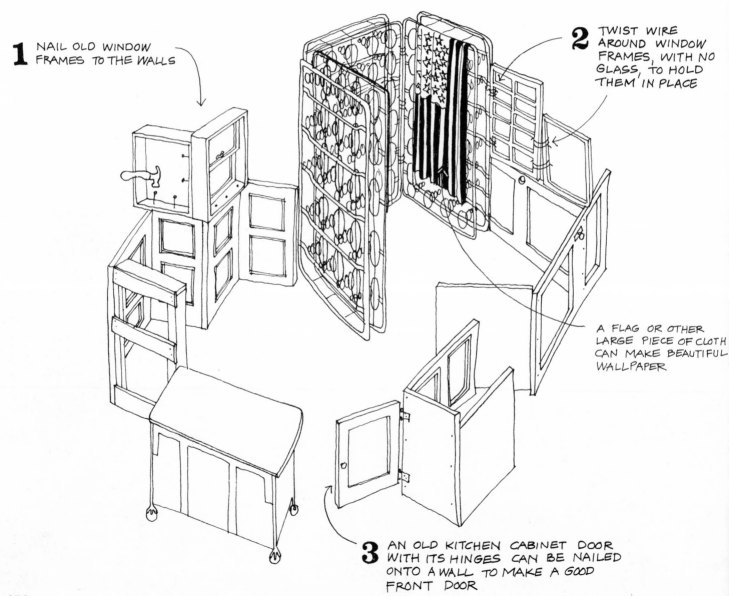

1 NAIL OLD WINDOW FRAMES TO THE WALLS

2 TWIST WIRE AROUND WINDOW FRAMES, WITH NO GLASS, TO HOLD THEM IN PLACE

A FLAG OR OTHER LARGE PIECE OF CLOTH CAN MAKE BEAUTIFUL WALLPAPER

3 AN OLD KITCHEN CABINET DOOR WITH ITS HINGES CAN BE NAILED ONTO A WALL TO MAKE A GOOD FRONT DOOR

Step 6
Building the Roof

Old doors make the best roofs for big rooms because they're strong. But you can use all sorts of things, like stretched cloth or plastic sheets, a beach umbrella, plywood, even tree branches and leaves for the roof.

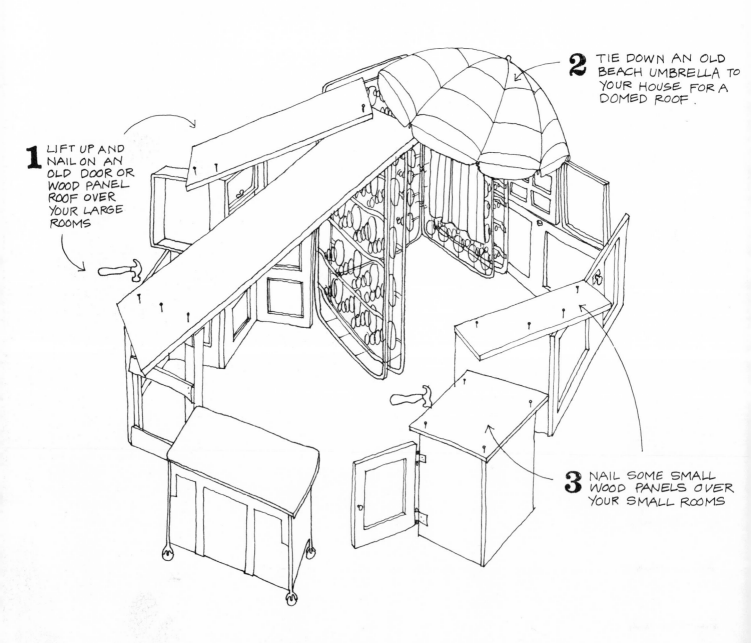

1 LIFT UP AND NAIL ON AN OLD DOOR OR WOOD PANEL ROOF OVER YOUR LARGE ROOMS

2 TIE DOWN AN OLD BEACH UMBRELLA TO YOUR HOUSE FOR A DOMED ROOF.

3 NAIL SOME SMALL WOOD PANELS OVER YOUR SMALL ROOMS

Step 7
Installing the Appliances & Furniture

You'll really have to use your imagination to furnish the house. Remember: almost any piece of junk can turn into something you need. Here are a few suggestions:

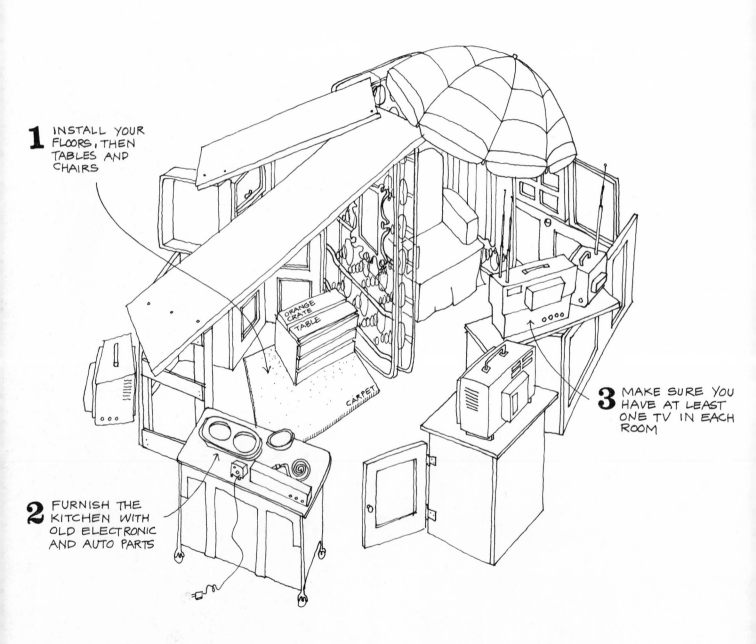

1 INSTALL YOUR FLOORS, THEN TABLES AND CHAIRS

ORANGE CRATE TABLE

CARPET

2 FURNISH THE KITCHEN WITH OLD ELECTRONIC AND AUTO PARTS

3 MAKE SURE YOU HAVE AT LEAST ONE TV IN EACH ROOM

The Tree House

The tree house is the place that gets you up off the ground and gives you an exciting bird's-eye view of things. It can make a great secret club house or hiding place. But, of course, you'll need a tree.

As you look for a tree, try to find one with at least 2 or 3 branches separated from the main trunk. These branches should be at least 10'' thick.

Next trim away the dead branches and clear an area for building. Always be careful not to harm the tree. Don't strip any bark or cut away any large live branches.

Now you're ready to build your tree house.

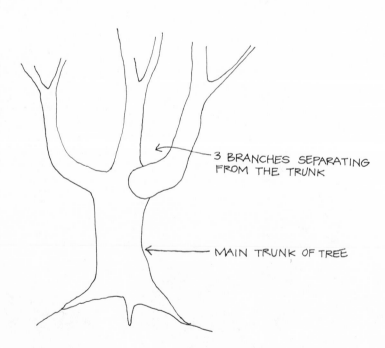

3 BRANCHES SEPARATING FROM THE TRUNK

MAIN TRUNK OF TREE

Step 1
Assembling the Tools

Gather the tools listed below on your workbench before beginning. This way, your work won't be interrupted because you have to find a tool.

1 HAMMER
FOR NAILING

2 CROSSCUT SAW
FOR CUTTING THE WOOD
TO THE RIGHT LENGTH

3 LEVEL
FOR LEVELING THE BEAMS
SO THAT THE HOUSE IS
STRAIGHT

4 SQUARE
FOR MAKING A PERPENDICULAR
LINE ON WOOD THAT IS TO BE SAWED

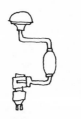

5 BRACE AND BIT
FOR DRILLING HOLES
FOR THE LADDER RUNGS

6 TAPE
FOR MEASURING
THE MATERIALS TO
THE RIGHT SIZE

7 BANDAGES
FOR CUTS

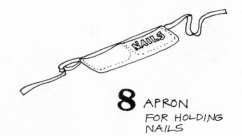

8 APRON
FOR HOLDING
NAILS

Step 2
Assembling the Materials

Here's a list of materials you'll need to build the tree house. You'll be able to buy them all at your lumber yard except the cloth, which can be bought at a fabric store. Make sure to get the lumber yard to saw the plywood sheet into the parts you'll need. This will save you some hard sawing work.

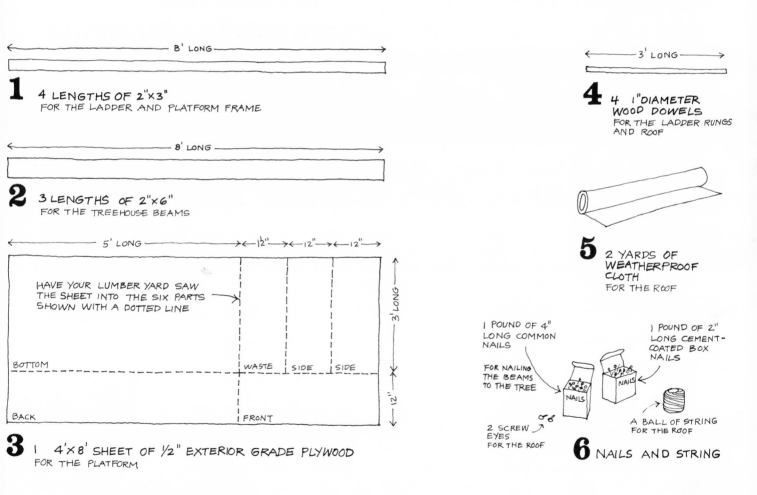

1 4 LENGTHS OF 2"X3"
FOR THE LADDER AND PLATFORM FRAME

2 3 LENGTHS OF 2"X6"
FOR THE TREEHOUSE BEAMS

3 1 4'X8' SHEET OF ½" EXTERIOR GRADE PLYWOOD
FOR THE PLATFORM

HAVE YOUR LUMBER YARD SAW THE SHEET INTO THE SIX PARTS SHOWN WITH A DOTTED LINE

BOTTOM   WASTE SIDE SIDE

BACK   FRONT

4 4 1"DIAMETER WOOD DOWELS
FOR THE LADDER RUNGS AND ROOF

5 2 YARDS OF WEATHERPROOF CLOTH
FOR THE ROOF

1 POUND OF 4" LONG COMMON NAILS
FOR NAILING THE BEAMS TO THE TREE

1 POUND OF 2" LONG CEMENT-COATED BOX NAILS

A BALL OF STRING
FOR THE ROOF

2 SCREW EYES
FOR THE ROOF

6 NAILS AND STRING

Step 3
Building the Ladder

Saw the steps of the ladder from the wood dowels. Ladder steps are called rungs. They fit tightly into the holes you drill into the ladder sides. You may have to hammer hard to get them all the way into the hole. To get a straight ladder, drill your holes into the ladder sides very straight. Take your time as you drill.

When you're forcing the second ladder side over the seven rungs, begin by hammering the first rung into its hole, then the second, and so on up the ladder.

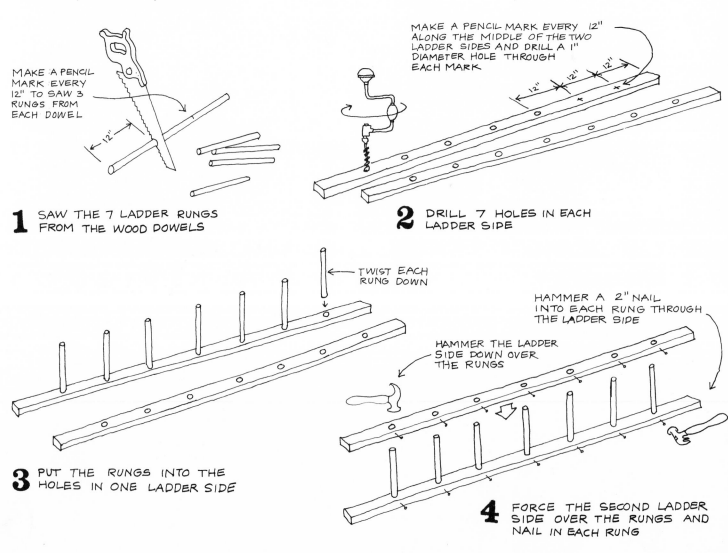

MAKE A PENCIL MARK EVERY 12" TO SAW 3 RUNGS FROM EACH DOWEL

12"

MAKE A PENCIL MARK EVERY 12" ALONG THE MIDDLE OF THE TWO LADDER SIDES AND DRILL A 1" DIAMETER HOLE THROUGH EACH MARK

12"   12"   12"

1 SAW THE 7 LADDER RUNGS FROM THE WOOD DOWELS

2 DRILL 7 HOLES IN EACH LADDER SIDE

TWIST EACH RUNG DOWN

HAMMER A 2" NAIL INTO EACH RUNG THROUGH THE LADDER SIDE

HAMMER THE LADDER SIDE DOWN OVER THE RUNGS

3 PUT THE RUNGS INTO THE HOLES IN ONE LADDER SIDE

4 FORCE THE SECOND LADDER SIDE OVER THE RUNGS AND NAIL IN EACH RUNG

Step 4
Building the Platform

The platform will be the floor of the tree house so it must be strong. As shown below, saw 2 of the 8' long 2"x3"s into frame pieces that will be nailed under the plywood to make a strong platform.

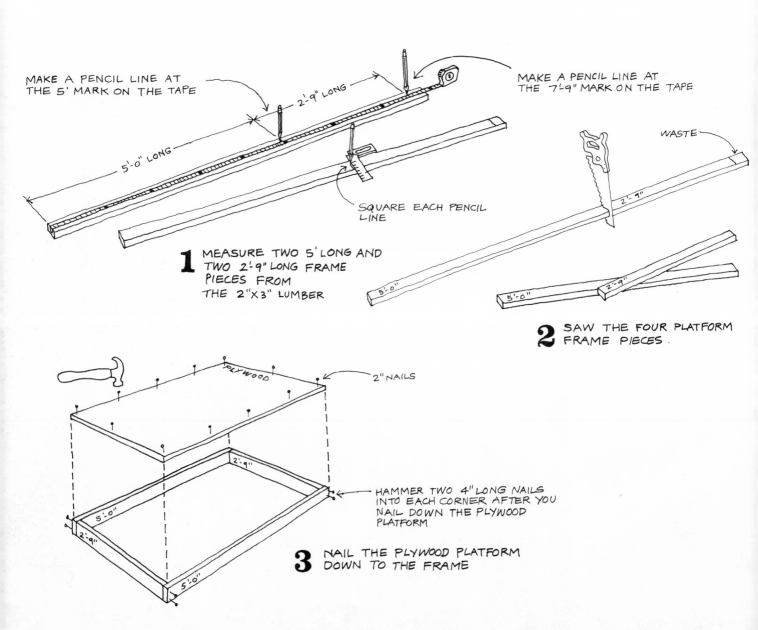

MAKE A PENCIL LINE AT THE 5' MARK ON THE TAPE

2'-9" LONG

MAKE A PENCIL LINE AT THE 7'-9" MARK ON THE TAPE

5'-0" LONG

SQUARE EACH PENCIL LINE

WASTE

2'-9"

1 MEASURE TWO 5' LONG AND TWO 2'-9" LONG FRAME PIECES FROM THE 2"X3" LUMBER

5'-0"

5'-0"   2'-9"

2 SAW THE FOUR PLATFORM FRAME PIECES.

PLYWOOD

2" NAILS

2'-9"

5'-0"

2'-9"

5'-0"

HAMMER TWO 4" LONG NAILS INTO EACH CORNER AFTER YOU NAIL DOWN THE PLYWOOD PLATFORM

3 NAIL THE PLYWOOD PLATFORM DOWN TO THE FRAME

Step 5
Nailing the Beams to the Tree

Nailing the beams to the tree is easy but you'll need a friend. Start by having your friend hold one end of the first beam until it is level. Then you nail it to the tree. The rest of your beams are nailed to the tree the same way. But, remember to make sure that all the beams are even with each other. After they are nailed in place, they will make a frame to hold the platform, so they must be level.

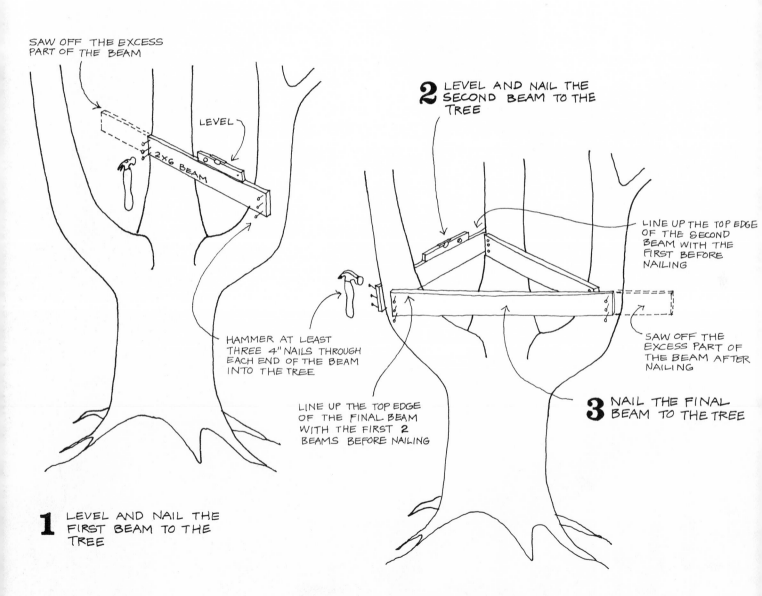

SAW OFF THE EXCESS PART OF THE BEAM

LEVEL

2×6 BEAM

2 LEVEL AND NAIL THE SECOND BEAM TO THE TREE

LINE UP THE TOP EDGE OF THE SECOND BEAM WITH THE FIRST BEFORE NAILING

HAMMER AT LEAST THREE 4" NAILS THROUGH EACH END OF THE BEAM INTO THE TREE

LINE UP THE TOP EDGE OF THE FINAL BEAM WITH THE FIRST **2** BEAMS BEFORE NAILING

SAW OFF THE EXCESS PART OF THE BEAM AFTER NAILING

3 NAIL THE FINAL BEAM TO THE TREE

1 LEVEL AND NAIL THE FIRST BEAM TO THE TREE

Step 6
Attaching the Platform

The platform will weigh about 30 pounds so you'll need some help in getting it up onto the beams. Once you've lifted it up, push it around until you feel it is in a sturdy position, then hammer the nails through it into the beams.

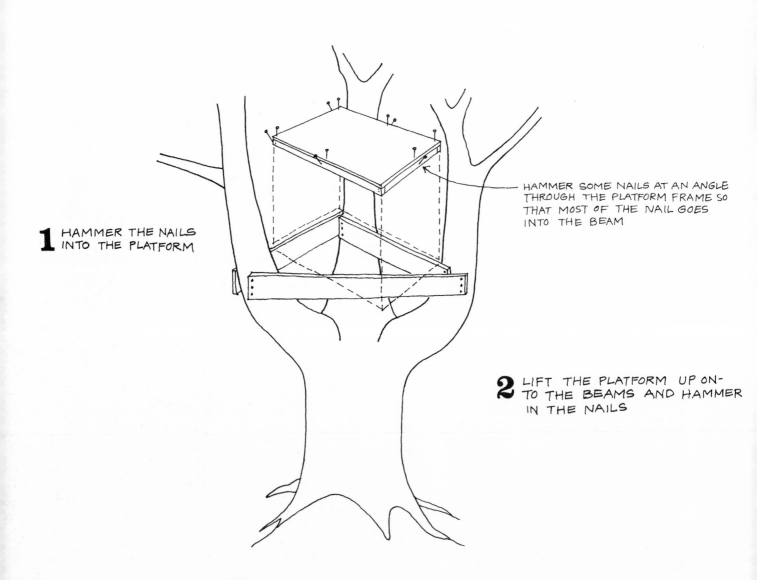

HAMMER SOME NAILS AT AN ANGLE THROUGH THE PLATFORM FRAME SO THAT MOST OF THE NAIL GOES INTO THE BEAM

1 HAMMER THE NAILS INTO THE PLATFORM

2 LIFT THE PLATFORM UP ONTO THE BEAMS AND HAMMER IN THE NAILS

Step 7
Attaching the Ladder and Sides

Have a friend hold the sides steady while you kneel on the platform and nail them into place. Make sure you line up the bottom edge of the sides with the bottom edge of the platform before you hammer in the nails. Lean the ladder up against the platform, making sure it's on firm ground before you nail it.

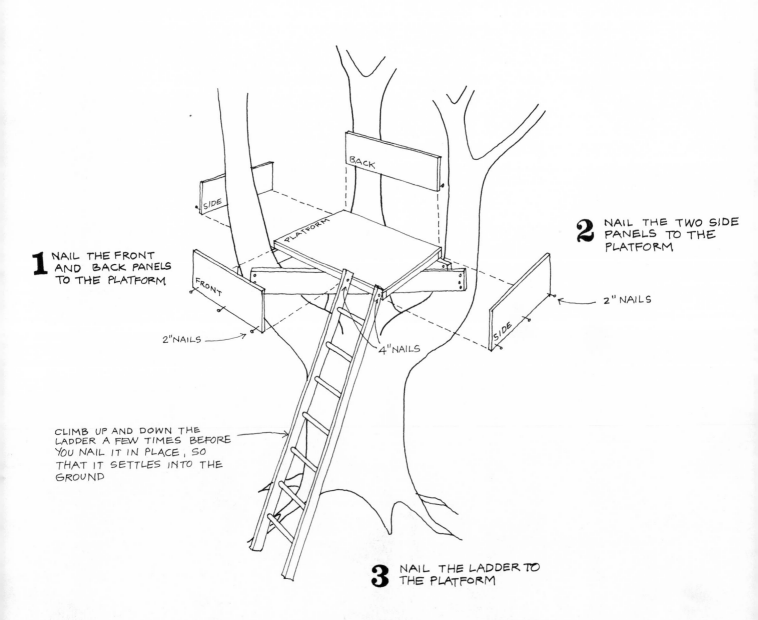

1 NAIL THE FRONT AND BACK PANELS TO THE PLATFORM

2 NAIL THE TWO SIDE PANELS TO THE PLATFORM

2" NAILS

2"NAILS

4"NAILS

CLIMB UP AND DOWN THE LADDER A FEW TIMES BEFORE YOU NAIL IT IN PLACE, SO THAT IT SETTLES INTO THE GROUND

3 NAIL THE LADDER TO THE PLATFORM

BACK

SIDE

PLATFORM

FRONT

SIDE

Step 8
Hanging the Roof

You may have to climb your tree to hang your roof high enough, so be careful. Tie all your knots very tight so that your roof doesn't blow away in a strong wind.

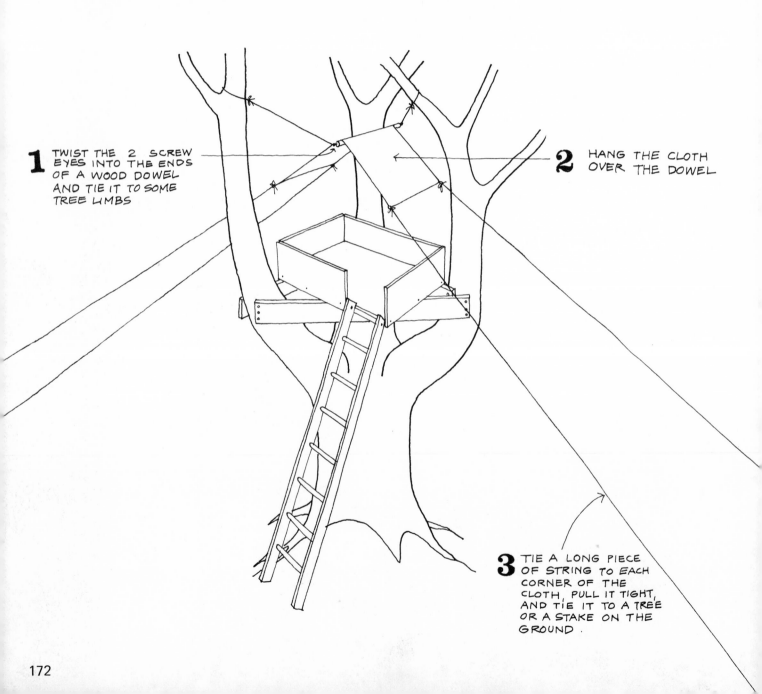

1 TWIST THE 2 SCREW EYES INTO THE ENDS OF A WOOD DOWEL AND TIE IT TO SOME TREE LIMBS

2 HANG THE CLOTH OVER THE DOWEL

3 TIE A LONG PIECE OF STRING TO EACH CORNER OF THE CLOTH, PULL IT TIGHT, AND TIE IT TO A TREE OR A STAKE ON THE GROUND.

Appendix

Illustrated Housebuilding
Graham Blackburn
Overlook Press
Lewis Hollow Road
Woodstock, New York 12498

A History of Prefabrication
Alfred Bruce and Harold Sandbank
Arno Press
330 Madison Avenue
New York, New York 10017

Energy Primer
Portola Institute
558 Santa Cruz Avenue
Menlo Park, California 94025

Build Your Own Early American Village
Forrest Wilson
Pantheon Books c/o Random House, Inc.
457 Hohn Rd.
Westminster, Maryland 21157

Shelter
Shelter Publications
Mountain Books
P.O. Box 4811
Santa Barbara, California 93103

Stanley Tools Company
600 Myrtle Street
New Britain, Connecticut 06050

Disston Tools Company, Inc.
Danville, Virginia 24541